SOMETHING ABOUT SILVER

SEAL Brotherhood: Silver Team
Book 1

SHARON HAMILTON

SHARON HAMILTON'S BOOK LIST

SEAL BROTHERHOOD BOOKS

SEAL BROTHERHOOD SERIES
Accidental SEAL Book 1

Fallen SEAL Legacy Book 2

SEAL Under Covers Book 3

SEAL The Deal Book 4

Cruisin' For A SEAL Book 5

SEAL My Destiny Book 6

SEAL of My Heart Book 7

Fredo's Dream Book 8

SEAL My Love Book 9

SEAL Encounter Prequel to Book 1

SEAL Endeavor Prequel to Book 2

Ultimate SEAL Collection Vol. 1 Books 1-4 /
2 Prequels

Ultimate SEAL Collection Vol. 2 Books 5-9

SEAL BROTHERHOOD LEGACY SERIES
Watery Grave Book 1

Honor The Fallen Book 2

Grave Injustice Book 3

Deal With The Devil Book 4

Cruisin' For Love Book 5

Destiny of Love Book 6

Heart of Gold Book 7

Father's Dream Book 8

Second Time Love Book 9

Little Miracles Novella

SEAL BROTHERHOOD SILVER TEAM SERIES

Something About Silver Book 1

BAD BOYS OF SEAL TEAM 3 SERIES

SEAL's Promise Book 1

SEAL My Home Book 2

SEAL's Code Book 3

Big Bad Boys Bundle Books 1-3

BAND OF BACHELORS SERIES

Lucas Book 1

Alex Book 2

Jake Book 3

Jake 2 Book 4

Big Band of Bachelors Bundle

BONE FROG BROTHERHOOD SERIES

New Year's SEAL Dream Book 1

SEALed At The Altar Book 2

SEALed Forever Book 3

SEAL's Rescue Book 4

SEALed Protection Book 5

Bone Frog Brotherhood Superbundle

BONE FROG BACHELOR SERIES
Bone Frog Bachelor Book 0.5
Unleashed Book 1
Restored Book 2
Revenge Book 3
Legacy Book 4

SUNSET SEALS SERIES
SEALed at Sunset Book 1
Second Chance SEAL Book 2
Treasure Island SEAL Book 3
Escape to Sunset Book 4
The House at Sunset Beach Book 5
Second Chance Reunion Book 6
Love's Treasure Book 7
Finding Home Book 8
Sunset SEALs Duet #1
Sunset SEALs Duet #2

LOVE VIXEN
Bone Frog Love

SHADOW SEALS
Shadow of the Heart
Shadow Warrior

SILVER SEALS SERIES
SEAL Love's Legacy

Heavenly Lover Book 1
Underworld Lover Book 2
Underworld Queen Book 3
Redemption Book 4

FALL FROM GRACE SERIES
Gideon: Heavenly Fall

SUNSET BEACH SERIES
I'll Always Love You
Back To You

NOVELLAS
SEAL Of Time: Trident Legacy

All of Sharon's books are available on Audible,
narrated by the talented J.D. Hart.

ABOUT THE BOOK

A relentless sniper, a love once lost, and a battle-scarred SEAL at a crossroads...

Harper Cunningham, a seasoned member of SEAL Team 3, thrives in the brotherhood of the battlefield but shuns the mantle of leadership after clashes with high-ranking officers. His heart, buried under the scars of war, still mourns Lydia, the woman he loved and lost to a sniper's bullet in North Africa—a loss that haunts his every mission.

Yet fate has a twist in store. Tasked with leading a special Silver Team, a unit of experienced SEALs, Harper is drawn into a high-stakes mission to preempt emerging terrorist threats. The mission takes an unexpected turn when he uncovers a startling truth: the sniper he killed in retribution was the wrong man.

As Harper navigates this dangerous new landscape, a stunning revelation upends his world—Lydia is alive. Torn between the path of revenge and the rekindling of an old flame, Harper stands at a crossroads, where every choice leads to irrevocable consequences. In this high-octane tale of loyalty, betrayal, and undying love, will Harper find his way to redemption, or will the shadows of the past consume his future?

Follow Harper in Book 1 of Sharon Hamilton's brand new SEAL Brotherhood series, with a whole new cast of characters, and the emergence of many you've loved from her past stories.

AUTHOR'S NOTE

I always dedicate my SEAL Brotherhood books to the brave men and women who defend our shores and keep us safe. Without their sacrifice and that of their families—because a warrior's fight always includes his or her family—I wouldn't have the freedom and opportunity to make a living writing these stories. They sometimes pay the ultimate price so we can debate, argue, go have coffee with friends, raise our children, and see them have children of their own.

One of my favorite tributes to warriors resides on many memorials, including one I saw honoring the fallen of WWII on an island in the Pacific:

> "When you go home
> Tell them of us, and say,
> For your tomorrow,
> We gave our today."

These are my stories created out of my own imagination. Anything that is inaccurately portrayed is either my mistake or done intentionally to disguise something I might have overheard over a beer or in the corner of one of the hangouts along the Coronado Strand.

I support two main charities. Navy SEAL/UDT Museum operates in Ft. Pierce, Florida. Please learn about this wonderful museum, all run by active and former SEALs and their friends and families, and who rely on public support, not that of the United States Government.

www.navysealmuseum.org

IF YOU GOT ANY CLOSER, YOU WOULD HAVE TO ENLIST

I also support Wounded Warriors, who tirelessly bring together the warrior as well as the family members who are just learning to deal with their soldier's condition and have nowhere to turn. It is a long path to becoming well, but I've seen first-hand what this organization does for its warriors and the families who love them. Please give what your heart tells you is right. If you cannot give, volunteer at one of the many service centers all over the United States. Get involved. Do something meaningful for someone who gave so much of themselves, to families who have paid the price for your freedom. You'll find a family there unlike any other on the planet.

www.woundedwarriorproject.org

CHAPTER 1

NAVY SEAL HARPER Cunningham sometimes came back from his SEAL Team 3 deployments and stayed a couple of days in the Coronado area with his best friend and fellow SEAL, Hamish McDougall. Hamish was on SEAL Team 5. The two were on opposite rotations, so Hamish was usually home, getting ready to do a work up for their next tour, when Harper returned. Both teams worked the same field: the Mediterranean and Northern Africa to the bulge, parts of Spain, and the Canaries.

Today, Harper wanted to go straight home—a long ten-hour drive up California's valley interior from Coronado to Sonoma County. He frequently made it in less than nine hours, reaching speeds of over 100 MPH.

Today, there was some urgency to his trip. He'd gotten a message from his father's doctor that his dad was having some difficulties in the hospital where he resided. Harper had sent him to live there when he became too difficult to handle, especially while Harper was on deployments.

The message was somewhat cryptic, yet Harper knew better than to try to reach the doctor.

When his wife, Lydia, had been alive, she would've gladly taken care of his dad and known exactly how to handle his outbursts stemming from his fears while losing his memory. Dementia ran in their family, Harper had learned by doing some research. He knew the signs of dementia were increasing every day, and there probably had been some kind of an incident— not life-threatening or the doctor would have said so. Nonetheless, it needed his immediate attention.

Putting it off a day or two—even though his body, his mind, his heart, and his eyes desperately needed rest and mindless beach time or buddy brews, anything other than focusing on solving some problem or emergency while running onto the battlefield— wouldn't work. Duty and guilt at not being there when his father had one of his meltdowns, now becoming more frequent, required he do everything humanly possible to protect his dad and restore his dad's world to calm and peace.

It was a battle of another sort, one his father was eventually going to lose, and probably soon.

Harper was full of pride at always being at the ready, no matter what. He didn't spend a second feeling sorry for himself or wishing it wasn't his lot in life. He reminded himself it was an honor that he had his dad, his only living relative after his mother's suicide ten years ago.

He churned in his seat, allowing his back to pop then slowly flexing and releasing his thighs one at a time. He drove through cities and both tiny and large rural farming towns, where cowboy boots were used for work and not for looks, where hats were always dirty unless attending church or walking into the bank for a loan, which he'd done with his father many times. The farmlands were dusty. The old orchards, now brown and twisted, looked like the dark forest in the *Wizard of Oz*, holding boarded-up farmhouses and old childless swings hanging by one chain from a large tree in the front yard.

It was evidence that life either moved on and survived elsewhere or didn't survive at all. Either way, it was sad to watch it spinning by his windows.

He felt sorry for the demise of the farming industry in California, felled by the politics of the Colorado River dispute, when the farmers lost to the development needs in LA and to the environmentalists in the North.

They never had a chance.

He stopped for fuel along the way, his four-door three-quarter ton diesel pickup getting almost twenty-five miles an expensive gallon. He munched on burgers he'd sorely missed on their last deployment to Africa, thick chocolate milkshakes, and, of course, coffee. He always loaded up on two or three tumblers of coffee, doctored with about a half pint of cream between them. He always ran out of cream and snap pickles or olives between fill-ups.

In those days, back when he had a wife and experienced three miraculous years he thought he'd never have, he never had problems with his dad because she knew how to charm the pants off the old guy, even though he was known for being fresh with the staff. It didn't matter how many times they told him, due to his dementia, he never remembered and most everyone laughed it off. He was never mean, just inappropriate. That was a constant problem.

But Lydia could handle it all. She had never complained. She was an angel in every sense of the word. His dad had no long-term cognition she was gone, just kept drifting off into space more and more frequently—his way of dealing with anything he didn't know how to take care of. He retreated more to his room and, of late, more to his TV while in bed.

"It's not fair to blame Lydia. Not fair at all. You stop that, Harper," he whispered to himself.

The love of his life and his only reason for living had been dead now nearly two years, shot by a sniper in Africa. And although Harper had been itching to go overseas on deployment at the same time as her, where they could share some of that time together, her nursing mission to a small village in Benin had popped up ahead of time. He had been nowhere near where she was to rescue her.

It was one of the biggest regrets of his life.

Four months later, as luck would have it, he got the opportunity to take down the guy who took that fatal shot. That in itself was satisfaction.

But it no way stopped the pain or regret. He'd failed to protect her. He'd known she shouldn't have gone by herself. The medical staff who accompanied her were not even shooters, and they only used local police for protection.

Still, it was his fault, because he couldn't convince her not to go. He didn't have the conversation skills Lydia had. Oh man, she could talk him into anything. She was so good.

That round should have hit his chest, not hers. It should have ended his life. His dad would be better off with Lydia, anyway. Harper knew that even his dog, Venom, had liked her more, and Venom had been so highly trained and was so loyal to Harper to begin with. It mattered little. Lydia wrapped them both around her little finger, and she'd always got her way.

He'd tried everything he could to get sent over early, but the Navy wasn't having any of it.

Yes, the world would now be a much better place if he could have Lydia back. He'd have given his own life if he could save her. But that wasn't to be.

He thought about Hamish and his little family, happily married, with children and grandchildren overrunning his quaint house he shared with his wife of thirty years. They had more dogs than Coronado allowed, and he was always getting in trouble for it. Harper envied him.

But Hamish was a different man. Every bit as courageous as Harper. He could settle down and be that kind of a family man. Harper was so discriminating he usually sent women screaming in the opposite direction, calling him all kinds of names he didn't like to hear and knew were untrue.

He was just unlucky with women. Until he met Lydia.

She'd been one of his dad's pretty nurses at the hospital after he'd fallen and injured himself in the care home. She stayed up with him and tended to him, probably wiping his butt and changing his diaper, although Lydia never told Harper that. She looked in on his dad so when Harper came to visit she had a full report ready for him without him even asking.

Hadn't taken long before he realized Lydia was sweet on him. Harper hadn't known what to do and figured she'd just talk herself out of it, like all the other ladies who came before. It was only going to be a matter of time. But, and as miraculous as it was, she finally approached him in the hallway one evening after she tended to his dad and his visit was concluded. It was late, very few staff on hand to overhear her soft whisper.

"So, Harper, when are you going to kiss me? I know you want to. Do I have to wait another few months or a year or two or a decade? What's your timing on all this?" she asked him.

That threw him off base big time.

"Timing? I don't usually think about timing when it comes to dating or… well, and especially about kissing women." He followed it up with an uncomfortable nervous smile and a chuckle.

Truth was, he was embarrassed.

"Come on, Harper. You're going to make me wait and wait and wait? You've already made me ask you. What more do you want?"

Harper didn't dare to scan her body from her head to her toes like he wanted to, but he saw her wonderful physique, ample bosom, and awesome ass in his mind, in his dreams every night before he went to bed. He easily recalled every luscious curve and wiggle, even the parts that jiggled a little bit, which kind of gave him an extra thrill.

"Oh, I could think of a lot of things you could do for me. I have a great imagination," he said and involuntarily blushed like a schoolgirl.

Goddammit.

"And here I thought you were a real man, Harper," she quickly replied.

"Oh, I am."

He stepped closer to her, put his hands under her chin, and lip-locked with her until he could feel her getting weak at the knees. She began to shake. He didn't let her go yet and deepened his kiss, inserting his tongue and letting her know exactly how wonderful she tasted, letting the flow of his emotions wash into her so she could experience how much he needed her.

It was even more than that, though. She was a good person. She was a beautiful woman—full of prowess, strength, athleticism. She was kind and calm.

And she was perfect for him. Someone capable of smoothing out all his rough edges—scars filled with loneliness and scenes of death and destruction.

They parted, and she brushed the hairs from her forehead, her eyelids fluttering. Her cheeks were bright red. "Wow!"

"Does that tell you I'm ready?"

She giggled and stared at her white clogs then met his gaze bravely. "I can see that you are. Now I have to ask myself if I am."

When they'd started dating, she teased him, inviting him to kiss her, hold her hand, brush his fingers through her hair, and squeeze and massage her back and arms. However, he stayed away from her female parts out of respect for Lydia. He didn't want to do what he'd done to so many women, even women who said they wanted it fast and hard. He was through doing that. He was forty years old, for chrissakes, and that's not how a forty-year-old man was supposed to treat a lady. She was fifteen years his junior, unmarried, maybe not fully available, either. He hadn't asked. He didn't want to know. But he guessed she wasn't the cheating kind so took it as a good sign that she'd wanted his first kiss and certainly hadn't objected to any of the ones that followed.

That summer was magic as they frolicked, walked through the vineyards, went wine tasting in Sonoma County, where both she and his father lived full-time. To Harper, it wasn't yet home. Not yet.

They went to the ocean and watched the waves crash upon the shore, laughed at sea lions, and occasionally spotted whales pass by on their journeys. They pretended they were tourists and dallied through little towns of Healdsburg, Sonoma, Kenwood, and Geyserville, picking out their favorite spots, indulging in gourmet foods and cheeses, and doing all the things tourists spent thousands and thousands of dollars doing.

Except she stayed in her little apartment on the square in Healdsburg, and he went home to his own place. He played it respectful. He was hoping she would soon move for a change.

He didn't have to wait long.

Within a month, she invited him to stay over one night, and it was just as he imagined. Her soft body and moans egged him on such that he felt like he was turning inside out with desire he could never fully satisfy. He could hardly wait to penetrate her, to fill her, to show her what it was like to be worshiped by a man.

He was fairly certain, by the way her large brown eyes widened with surprise as he loved her with everything he had, that she had never really experienced that before.

They made love several times that night, and as sunrise dawned through the tall wooden windows, softened by the white gauzy curtains that floated in the breeze, he was hooked. He was completely hooked and was not the same man in the morning that he had been last night.

Suddenly, he knew what it was like to be addicted to cocaine or some kind of substance, even alcohol. This was better than any of that. She was his elixir, the beginning of his life at forty years of age. He'd waited a long time to find someone like her, someone patient, someone who didn't show him she needed him until he was deep inside her, rooting and kissing, biting her ear, as she squeezed his buttocks and arched to receive him as fully and deeply as she could.

That's when he knew she was hooked as well.

As he neared Sonoma County, he thought about the first day he brought her to his little house. It was a choice piece of property in between Santa Rosa and Sonoma. Nestled in the hills, he had the option of going east into the Sonoma Square proper or west into downtown Santa Rosa and the Russian River and coast beyond. His property had a view of everything from Sebastopol North all the way to Cloverdale and beyond, up the hill and over the canyon. From the second story of his home, he could see the park in Bennett Valley and the hidden lake he liked to run and hike through when he was home.

His father now lived on the other side of the hill in the converted mental hospital turned into a Veterans dementia treatment facility, called Valley of the Moon Veterans Home.

The day he brought her to the house, he opened the door, let her inside first, then followed behind. When she entered, his whole life changed. The house took on a glow he'd never felt or seen before. She had transformed every living and nonliving thing around her just by being there—even the floors, the doors she opened. She stepped out onto the patio and looked at the flowers he had planted in wooden container boxes, along with his fresh vegetables and herbs. She let her fingers glide over the tops of the old-fashioned metal rocking chairs, viewing the meadow in front of her. She silently took in the scenery and inhaled then turned to give him a smile.

"It's breathtaking, Harper. I've never been up in these hills before. You have a piece of paradise here."

"That's what I thought too. I bought it off an old farmer who retired here. He was going to put in a vineyard, but his wife passed away. He never got around to it and finally decided he couldn't live here anymore without her, so he sold it to me. He told me I would find myself a better person by living here."

"But you work in Coronado. You work on the Teams, right?"

They had discussed this before. "Yes. My father and mother lived downtown in Santa Rosa, and I was raised here in my high school years. I've been all over the world, of course, and most of my friends live down in Coronado. When I'm home, I come back up here to visit my dad. It's a nice place to come back to—no battleships like some of the houses and apartments down there. No Navy jets. No men running on the beach. Party central downtown, bonfires in Coronado.

I just like it here. And this is good for his dementia. Up until a few months ago, he lived with me here. Two cranky bachelors. Now I've got him in the Vets. It's a great place."

"I've heard good things about it." She stopped and studied everything again. "Well, it's just awesome. How many acres do you have?"

"Just shy of thirty acres. I'm having a hard time deciding what to do with it. I'm not really a farmer, but I do like to garden a little bit for my own food when I can. I've got some neighbors down the driveway. Sally, down about a half mile away, takes care of Venom when I'm gone. Today, he's at the vet. They'll be here shortly. He got a little cut on his paw."

"Venom?" she asked.

"My dog. He's a champion European black Doberman. He looks fierce as hell, but he's a sweetheart really. I think he'll like you."

"I'm sure he will. I love dogs, and they can tell. I've never been around a Doberman, so you'll have to teach me."

He walked over to her slowly and, with the gentle breeze blowing through her hair, laced his fingers through it, noting all the red highlights in her dark brown color, her strands so shiny he could almost see his face in it. He leaned down very carefully and lifted her up with both arms around her so that she could encircle his waist, her arms tucked around his neck.

He bent down and kissed her. Then he kissed her down the side of her neck and nuzzled between the buttons on the front of her shirt.

Holding her gently, he slowly walked her inside, closing the door behind them and taking her to the bedroom. He stopped in front of the bed.

"This is my sanctuary. I have never had a woman here. I've never entertained anyone in the bedroom. My neighbor has been in the house, of course, but I've never ever had anyone here. You're the first."

Her body slipped down his frontside, over his hardness until her feet touched the floor. She stayed pressed against him, her arms still crisscrossed behind his neck.

"The first, huh? Somehow, I thought you'd be way more experienced." She smiled.

"Well, I guess it doesn't show, does it? Yeah, I'm experienced all right, but not when it comes to this."

She studied his face carefully. "And what *is* this?"

"I don't know, Lydia. But whatever it is, I don't want it to end. Ever."

And that was how it had been. That first day. Those first few precious steamy hours in the middle of the late morning. The first time he tried to convince her through the movements of his body that she was home, he would protect her, and he never wanted her to leave.

He would devote his entire life to making her happy.

But, of course, those words could not be spoken yet. That was yet to come.

CHAPTER 2

HARPER GAVE SALLY a call to let her know he'd made it to Sonoma County but was going to visit his dad first. He'd stop by and pick up Venom afterward.

"I can just leave him in the house, if you want me to," Sally answered. "You know I have a key."

"Thank you, but I don't know how long it's going to be, and unless you object to me getting there after midnight, I prefer he stay with you."

"Fine by me. He's sitting right in front of me, patiently waiting. He's listening and hearing your voice. Anxiously waiting. I'm sure he's happy about that. He's such a good boy, but he missed you this time."

Harper was used to spending hours staring into the soulful eyes of his best friend, the one who was always happier to see him the later he was. Unlike human friends, who might feel slighted, he was just delighted with every bit of attention Harper could give him. And there were some days when Harper was so wrought with pain, he hardly paid attention to the world at all.

The veterans home was always lit impressively, having been built in the early 1900s. It was of Spanish Rococo design with fake urns and cherubs, which adorned the large archway entrance to the administration center where he had to check in. The building was huge. The two-story dorms on the sides were a later addition, more modern and built in the 1950s. Built for function, they were extremely ugly and "cake-box" looking.

The old part of the hospital was surrounded by little cottages that had housed teams of doctors who'd lived on campus while they ministered to the mentally ill population, mostly deaf and Down's syndrome patients. This had been considered a perk that made it possible to find some of the very best doctors in the country. All that changed as their patients aged out. Then the facility was shut down and lay dormant for a time. The Veterans Administration purchased the property around the year 2000 and began fixing the disrepair, building by building, as money was raised.

The color of the plaster reminded Harper of Spanish Revival buildings in the San Diego area or places he'd seen in Arizona. The light warm sandstone color contrasted beautifully with the bright blue California sky during the day, with arched windows and walkways, ornate trim, and oversized tall ceilings that stretched up more than twenty feet on the ground floor. Tonight, floodlights illuminated the façade like an old Hollywood studio.

Money was always an issue, Harper remembered as he recalled the history of the property. It was expensive to maintain with all the little things always going wrong. The interior of the administration center was furnished with older leather furniture, antique tables, and hand-me-downs brought by families of veterans who stayed there. It reminded him of an old Boy Scout retreat he'd seen somewhere.

In the old days, the facility itself had a petting zoo, a farm for raising meat, a big garden, and an orchard where the patients used to work. They raised all their own food and for many, many years were self-sustaining.

Referencing newly enacted child labor laws, the state of California put a stop to all that. But Harper knew where all the orchards were at the top of the hill, branches still reaching to the sky, working hard to produce oranges, cherries, pears, apples, and nectarines. There were even some walnut trees there. No one had pruned them for probably thirty years or more. No one sprayed them, but the fruit came anyway. And what managed to grow was small and spotted but pretty good. He had taken his dad up there on several occasions, and they brought back baskets of summer fruits for the staff and patients to enjoy.

The attendant at the front desk notified the staff on his father's floor, and a heavyset nurse in a starched white uniform and bulky lace-up hospital shoes that squeaked appeared in front of him and gave him a firm and steady handshake.

"Mary. Evening supervisor."

"Nice to meet you, Mary. I'm Harper. How bad is it this time?"

She immediately looked at the floor and then side-glanced to view through the blackened windows to some imaginary green garden.

"I'm not going to lie to you, Mr. Cunningham. Your dad's too much for most of the female staff here to take care of. That and he seems to be regressing to something like teenage behavior. Difference is, he's strong and still runs when we get someone to accompany him. He works out like crazy, so he could easily overpower just about anybody here. He's fit otherwise. He might outlive us all yet!"

Harper chuckled at that, agreeing with her.

"Right now, he can be talked down out of things, and we are able to get close enough to him to give him medication to settle him down. But oh my gosh, the last two days have been pure Hell for all of us. I'm sure for him too."

"What happened?"

"Well, I don't know, but I think he was looking for you perhaps. He might've been looking for your mother? He was pacing the room, shouting things to himself over and over again, making little sense. He was missing *somebody*. Perhaps he was just lonely but didn't know how to deal with it."

"Did he get hurt or did he hurt anybody?"

"Not yet. But he is restrained in his bed. He didn't sleep last night at all—stayed awake, continuing on to today yelling and swearing at the top of his lungs. We finally sedated him about seven o'clock tonight. He's snoring up a storm now. When he wakes up, we'll see if sedation is needed again. I've had several other residents in the hall complain. At least he's asleep for now." She paused and carefully continued. "I'm just not sure this treatment, giving him access to run about the grounds, is good for him anymore. He could be a danger to himself as well as others."

Harper was distressed with the news. "Well, let me go see him. You want me to ask him some questions or you want me to just leave him alone if he's sleeping?"

"Let him sleep. But I want to show you some things he did. He made some drawings on the wall."

Good grief. Now what's he done?

"You want to tell me or just spring it on me?" Harper finally finished.

The nurse smiled behind her fingers, obviously feeling embarrassment. She whispered her answer out of earshot of the attendant at the desk, telling him, "I'll use his words. Tits and ass."

Evidently, her whisper carried farther than she'd calculated, because the receptionist looked up suddenly, staring back and forth between the two of them.

Harper chuckled. "I'm sure he has no idea what he's done."

"Oh, you're right, of course. It's just that it's bothering the other patients too. I hate to suggest it, but we have other rooms that are more like padded lockdowns, like a safe cell, but I know it would petrify him. If he can't be controlled, I'm afraid that's your only other alternative. I hate to see him lose his room and that view of the garden. As you know, he has some things from your old house and from your mother that are dear to him, when he is cogent."

"I get it. He spends most of his time being easy to work with, but he's putting everyone in the place to have to treat him as if he is mostly out of control. That's a shame. Let me see him. I'd like to schedule an appointment with Dr. Smiley as well."

"Yes, of course. I would never entertain any of this without his consultation. But I've heard him ponder how far gone he is. You need to know that."

"Thanks for the heads-up."

"He seems to especially enjoy his rocking chair."

"It was my mother's."

"Yes, he doesn't mention her by name any longer, but he loves sitting in it. He also enjoys sitting in his closet. He likes hanging up his robe, going to get his slippers, little routines like that."

Harper knew he liked those little routines. It gave him peace. As a boy, his father had all his fishing tackle so organized he could tell if Harper had stolen one of his lures or rummaged to look for hooks. It was the same thing for his tools in the garage. All the sharp edges faced the same direction; drawers were labeled and categorized by type of tool.

"Funny. He reminds me of me now. Not when I was a kid. I was never organized enough for him," he said.

"He insists on shaving when he can and enjoys the community of taking showers with the other residents. He seems to perk up with the men's locker room banter, like he felt he was playing football again in college. He has special buddies, teammates, he calls them. They sit in the card room. We don't allow smoking, but they ask every time and complain when they're denied. They talk about the old days."

"Navy guys. I'll bet he sticks to the Navy guys," Harper said.

"Oh, you got that right. The Navy guys kind of stay

together, and the Army guys stay together, and then we have others who served in the Corps. They blend in, but mostly, they stick to themselves. Some days, I feel so sorry for him, and for you too. We're going to have to figure this out."

It affected Harper more than he let on. He followed Mary down the hall, distracted by the quietness of the vinyl flooring, the occasional snoring he heard from various room doors left ajar, and her squeaking shoes, more on the right than the left, echoing off the wide hallways.

They rode the slow elevator to the second floor where his dad's room was. Three doors down, his father's name was printed on a cardboard hand-lettered plaque, adorned with an anchor at both sides.

She pushed open the wide wooden door, and they watched him sleeping on his back, mostly because the three-inch wide straps held him securely in place. Harper felt sorry for him, because he knew he'd never be able to sleep that way. He liked to toss and turn all night long. He knew his dad was unhappy just by looking at the expression on his face with his mouth wide-open, his brow curled in an angry grimace, and his hair disheveled.

Quietly, he tiptoed over to the side of the bed and said not a word, but he leaned over to study him more closely.

Harper observed his dad had cut himself shaving. Remnants of shaving cream were present on the cut with pieces of tissue attached to stop the bleeding. He had six or seven such areas peppering his cheeks and under his chin.

His father had lost several pounds since he'd last seen him. His cheeks were sunken, and his skin was a light shade of pinkish green. Harper pointed to the hallway indicating he wanted to ask Mary some questions.

But just at that moment, his dad's eyes opened wide. He gave his son a devilish grin. "Sonny! You came back!"

"Of course I did, Dad. I don't plan on dying in Africa."

"Africa? Beautiful place but very deadly. You know they have scenery there that I don't think you could see anywhere else in the world. Diamonds—they find diamonds when they farm, did you know that?"

Harper answered him. "Yes, Dad. I've seen them. I've seen the kids find them."

"They keep their teeth, not like in Europe. Weak teeth there. Awful teeth."

Harper completely agreed, laughing on the inside at his father's choice of subject matter.

"Have you seen the plains, Son? Beautiful golden fields in East Africa. Savannahs. Lots of wildlife. The

Mountains of the Moon! Have you gone hunting? They have great guides."

Harper had heard some wild stories about how several of his father's unit took a safari vacation to Kenya and all wound up in jail, nearly causing an international incident.

"They sure do have wild animals. We call them militia. They can't shoot worth a shit," Harper retorted.

His father seemed not to hear him. staring into the rocking chair as if someone sat there.

"Your mother was just here, Sonny. Looking radiant as always."

Harper turned to Mary, who nodded slowly, then studied her shoes patiently.

His dad had traveled all over the world. Before SEAL Teams were created, his father did a lot of underwater UDT missions, handling explosives and getting into dangerous underwater situations. The United States wasn't as heavily invested in Africa as European countries were, but once in a while, they would have to go in and evacuate villages. Medical staff were occasionally in danger. Well-meaning missionaries sometimes found themselves on the wrong end of somebody's rifle—which would make them on the wrong side of some warlord's world view. It never changed. In another one hundred years, he didn't think it would change at all.

"No, Dad, I haven't gone hunting. Something on my bucket list. Maybe you and I will go. We can go shoot some boar or deer if you like. How about it?"

"In Africa?"

Harper could see his eyes begin to fade, get glassy, and lose their focus. He was fading into some kind of alternative reality that wasn't going to allow his attention and focus.

"How are you feeling, Dad? I understand you've had some issues."

Without acknowledging Harper's question, his dad asked, "How long are you staying this time, Sonny? Oh, your mother's going to be so happy."

His mother was always good subject material, but as his dad's dementia came on, it was less and less likely he was ever going to face the fact that his wife was gone. He'd given up even trying to convince his dad of it.

"I made sure to give her a call so she knows I'll be coming," Harper played along.

"You're such a good boy. Hey, what do you want for Christmas? Do you want a bicycle, Sonny? They have some great bicycles down at the—what's the name of that store?"

"The Schwinn store?"

His dad didn't answer, again appearing not to hear. The store he was referring to was where he used to buy bicycles when he was in high school and had been closed for nearly twenty years. But Harper continued.

"You know, Dad, you bought me a nice one last year. I love that thing. I don't want to give it up for anything. So you just save your money."

His dad grinned, his face wrinkled in long lines along the sides of his eyes and cheeks, his mouth twisted and grooved from more laughter than frowns. Even as a boy, his dad had the Grand Canyon between his brows, and it was getting deeper still. His lips pulled back over his teeth, revealing how much his gums had receded. His lips were turning purple. Harper was going to have to ask about that.

"How are you feeling, Dad? Any problems?"

"Oh, I'll tell you this, Sonny, this is a great place. I'd come back here. They really take good care of me. I mean, I wish your mom was here too, but oh my gosh, I would come back again. Wonderful vacation. Wonderful people. And the music—they have a lot of talented people here. They sing, dance. We make music sometimes here with the buds. It's just a ball."

"I'm glad. I'm really glad."

Harper was suddenly tired and wanted to get home and get a good night's rest. He missed Venom and couldn't wait to see the beautiful dog.

"So, Dad, I'm going to take off, but I'll come back tomorrow, okay?"

"They might have space or could put you up in here. And let me tell you something, the girls here are fantastic! I mean, I've never seen such beautiful waitresses, just beautiful wait staff. Very efficient and the food is excellent. I'm going to book a nice, long massage!"

"Well, I don't want to spoil it for you then. I'll come back tomorrow, and we'll sit down and have a long talk. Maybe we'll go for a walk?"

"I would like that. How long are you staying this time?"

"I'm not sure. Maybe a couple of weeks. I have some work to do at the house, and then I have to return back south for a couple of Team meetings. But I'll be able to visit you several times. Don't worry."

"Then I'll have all the ladies to myself!"

Harper had turned to go when Mary pointed to the wall. Scrawled all over it in permanent black felt marker were pictures, just like she described. Cocks, tits, and ass. It appeared no one cleaned it up, fearing he'd just re-decorate the wall all over again.

He closed his eyes, opened them again, and still saw the vulgar images staring back at him. He was going to say something to his father about it, but the old man was staring out the black window at nothing.

CHAPTER 3

H ARPER DROVE SLOWLY up the two-mile paved road that led to Sally's house, about a mile from the top of the hill where Harper lived. There was a full moon outside, peeking out through the oak and madrone trees that hung over the driveway. In the midnight air, the forest was shiny with moisture picked up in the moonlight. When he rolled down the windows, he heard distant coyotes and predatory birds flying overhead, owls and hawks signaling to each other.

At Sally's front door, he heard her talking to Venom and the familiar tap-tap-tap of his claws on Sally's wooden floors. The dog was dancing in circles inside, Harper knew this. Of course Venom would recognize the sound of his truck, probably the sounds of his gait as he crunched his way across the gravel driveway as well. So when Harper knocked on the door and Sally opened it wide, Venom lunged into his arms, nearly tipping him backward off the front porch and onto his butt.

"Whoa, Boy. Missed you too, Bud," he said, laughing as the dog tried every way he could to lick his face.

The dog squealed then danced around him in circles. Jumping, he tried to lick his face again. Venom was filled with exuberance, showing Harper he was beyond delighted to see him again. If the dog had arms, Harper knew he would've returned the hug Harper gave him when he knelt and wrapped his arms around the dog's torso. Venom placed his large head on Harper's shoulder, leaning into his ear, and then reared back to lick his face.

Sally interceded on Harper's behalf. "Now, now Venom, let's calm down," she said. "He's been so excited, ever since the phone call. He's not been controllable."

As if to confirm, Venom leaned in and licked him on the lips all the way up his nose and between his eyebrows.

Harper laughed, trying to catch the dog again. "Well, I guess this can be excused. But you need to settle down, okay?"

Venom sat on his haunches and waited for a command. It was like he was demanding Harper tell him to do something and he would gladly do it, whether it was pick up a toy or fetch a stick or a ball or chase a critter. He was letting Harper know he was ready for action, and it mattered not that it was in the middle of the night.

Harper stood, adjusting his back while Venom turned toward Sally and sat on Harper's feet. They were one team, man and dog.

"Sorry about the late night, Sally. But I'm glad I saw Dad. I've got some things to research in the morning, and I'll have to go back there. He's okay for now, but man, I'm not sure how much longer all this is going to work."

Sally frowned, her grey hair disheveled as she wiped her hands on her apron. Her eyes showed nothing but compassion. She tilted her head to the side. "I'm so sorry, Harper. You don't need that complication, do you?"

"Timing's never good, Sally. Not when it comes to the end of life for someone you love. It's just the way it goes, isn't it? The hits keep on coming. Still, we all know his time is running out. The body is more than willing, and part of me wishes he wasn't so healthy." He gave Sally a big smile.

"Oh, I understand. And you know, sometimes they can last a long time but just get more and more difficult. You're back now. I'm sure you'll figure it out, Harper. You always do. How was your trip?"

"You mean, did I save the world?" he said, chuckling.

"Something like that, yes. I know you won't really tell me."

"It was good, intense like it always is. I'd like to think we're making a dent, eliminating some of the evildoers in the world, but as fast as we go after them, they recruit more, have more little bad guys. Teach them starting as toddlers to hate us and everything we stand for. I just do what I'm told. I wish I had a little more say so as to what our missions were. But I'm not complaining."

"As I recall, you didn't want any part of leadership, so I guess you get what you pay for, right?" she asked him.

"True. And I'd rather have it this way than being responsible for the whole team. I'm just not made out to be that kind of a leader. I can jump in and do things and be very present, but I really don't want to run anything. Those days are over, my friend."

"Makes it simpler. Some of the firms I've worked for, they have partners who get involved in every last detail from personnel issues to office policies. Honestly, getting a bunch of attorneys to agree to anything, well, it's impossible. It's like the way they run the government," Sally said with a shrug.

"The military too. None of us, none of our teams go unscathed. Is there ever a 'nice' way to go to war? To be protectors? We either do such a good job we get into trouble or not enough and get ourselves and our Teammates or hostages killed. Either way, there is no perfect solution, yet that's what we're tasked with—do it perfectly. Execute it exactly how it's supposed to be, when nothing works that way. Not ever, because the enemy always gets a vote."

"Well, Harper, I'm in your camp. I just do my own thing, and I guess I'm enough of an oddball they leave me alone. At least I get to take off when I want, take the cases I want to win. Venom and I went up to Mendocino for a weekend trip, and he loved it. Even likes the new car. It's beautiful up there. Bought some artwork and just enjoyed the scenery, the art galleries, the coffee shops, and little country stores and eateries."

Harper looked down at Venom, who was turning his head toward Sally and trying to figure out what she was saying. Then he focused on Harper, who bent over. "You go on a trip with Sally? You enjoy riding in the car?"

Venom stood, wagging his little stub of a tail and looking from Harper's face to Sally's. Harper knew he thought perhaps he was going to go for a car ride. The dog sat and barked one time. That was his signal for "yes."

"So is your dad otherwise doing well? How's his memory holding up overall?" asked Sally.

"No, it's getting worse each visit, but it was more

dramatic this time. He's lost a lot of weight, and he seems to be drifting off a little bit more. I'm embarrassed to say, he started drawing pornographic pictures on the wall with a felt marker, a *permanent* marker. I practically burst out laughing, except it'll cost us some serious dough to get that wall resurfaced and repainted. No sense doing it until he's done with his artistic phase," he answered.

Sally crossed her arms and shook her head. "Like you said, the hits just keep on coming. At least he's not lying there like a vegetable like so many people there at their end of days. That would be harder, I think. He's a rascal, but I guess that's where you get it, right?" She looked at him with the twinkle in her eye and a smile on her lips. "Speaking of which, I've got another prospect for you."

Sally was good at hooking Harper up with some of her lady friends. She even set up a blind date with him with one of her clients, until it went horribly wrong and she promised never to do that again. Harper was fairly sure Sally was gay, but they never discussed it, except they both liked looking at interesting, beautiful, and strong women. She never commented on men in that way.

"Sally, you know that never works out. I am done doing blind dates."

"Oh, you're going to like this one. She's a yoga instructor. Beautiful, slender, and graceful, she does yoga out at the beach. 'Yoga by Moonlight,' she calls it. A lot of couples go, not just women. I think you'd really like her. She's almost twenty years younger than you, in her mid-twenties, and she's got a figure that—well, she could be a model. And think about her flexibility, Harper."

Sally couldn't help but give him a wink.

Harper was embarrassed for her and saw that she was as well.

"Sally, do you think that's all I care about?"

"Oh, I hope it's something you care about, Harper. It's not right for a man like you, so handsome and full of life, to be single. I just think it would be a shame for you to miss out on some wonderful loving and nurturing times. There's got to be a woman out there somewhere who wants that, Harper. And it just breaks my heart to know that you aren't even trying. Unless you're getting sweet on men."

"Hardly, no offense."

"None taken."

"Sally, come on. You know there was only one woman for me."

"But until you met her, you didn't know that. And look, it happened. What's to say it couldn't happen again?"

"Because I'm not that lucky."

HE TOOK VENOM in the truck with him, cautiously driving up the rest of the driveway until they came to his electric gate. Punching the remote on his key fob, the gate drew back and lights turned on along the driveway and the front of the house. As he drove through into his inner sanctum, the gate closed behind him.

"We're home. I'll bet you're happy to be back here, right, Venom?"

The dog was sitting in the passenger seat, all nearly hundred pounds of him, erect, his ears pointed toward the ceiling, scanning the driveway and paying attention to any small critters that might chance invading their space. He looked at Harper and then searched the grounds. Looking off to the sides where, even though there was no light, he was able to see things in the woods surrounding them. Nothing of interest caught his eye.

Harper had pulled up to the garage and grabbed his keys. Venom followed him and waited by the front door. He punched in the alarm code and disabled the security system. Once he stepped inside, he stopped to see if he could detect anybody in the house, just a habit he'd always had. He didn't hear a sound or smell anything unusual. One time, he'd come home to find out he'd left a pot of water boiling, and it had completely smoked the house out.

This time, he smelled the candles, those frosty vanilla ones that Lydia liked so well, the scent of their wicks wafting through the air. He walked through the living room and into the kitchen, checked doors and windows downstairs, and then went back to the front door, locked his car remotely, and armed the whole perimeter.

With Venom behind him, he jogged upstairs to the bedroom and started stripping off his clothes, putting them in the laundry. He would get his duffel bag in the morning. Everything else he needed was at the house. His weaponry was locked in a bolted case underneath the front seat and would be safe for now. Besides, he had a small armory in the house he could use to defend against a significant militia attack.

On the bed was a note from Sally.

I know you told me not to do it, but I couldn't help myself. I came over and cleaned house this Friday, changed your sheets (not the special pillow), washed them, and put them back in your closet. I brought Venom with me, and he seemed to enjoy settling down on the couch or on your bed. I think he figured out that you would be home soon. Hope you forgive me.

Harper looked at Venom, who had already positioned himself on the bed, right in the middle between the two pillows. "So you helped Sally, did you? Did you learn how to vacuum?"

Venom angled his head again and perked his ears, then licked his nose, and waited for another question.

Harper continued on with the letter.

> *I have found you another prospect, and if I've seen you first before you get this message, you know all about her. But she's a beautiful young gal in her early twenties, really well put together, and has a yoga practice along the coast of our Bodega Bay. She does evening yoga classes on the beach at sunset. I have attached a schedule of her classes and her fees, but her beach yoga is free and open to all: beginner, intermediate and advanced.*
>
> *I think you should check her out.*
>
> *I know you don't want me to fix things up for you, so I haven't told her about you. That's different than before right? So no blind date! This is just a suggestion. I hope you take me up on it. I know a little bit of fun and relaxation in your life would do you good.*
>
> *All the best, Sally*

Harper knew Sally didn't date, although they'd never discussed her lack of having someone in her personal life. The issue just never came up. He figured she would tell him someday, and there was probably some kind of a sad story she didn't want to reveal yet. It was just a hunch.

Sally had lived in Sonoma County her whole life and had never traveled. She was dedicated to her work, settling custody and divorce issues. He knew all of her clients were extremely lucky to have her caring abilities to help them wade through a difficult time. He figured she was probably like him, a "one and done" type of gal.

He imagined he would never really get over Lydia, and he suspected perhaps Sally was also silently suffering the same fate. But he wasn't going to pry.

Examining the card Sally left, he noted she was right about one thing: the lady in the picture was extremely hot. But he wasn't ready for any of it.

He finished undressing, hopped into the shower, and took a long, steamy meditation there. Once done, he found Venom waiting for him beside his double sink and countertop. To the left was his sink where his toothbrush, favorite soaps, aftershave, and hand soap were stored underneath the mirror cabinet. On the right was Lydia's area. There was a pretty hand-painted flower drinking glass still with water in it halfway. It had been there two years, and somehow, still the water remained. Her toothbrush was still there next to the sink. Her hand towel hung in the ring underneath the medicine cabinet. He didn't even want to open it, knowing it was filled with some of her special things that made her so beautiful—her favorite perfumes, her vitamins, and her pills. He wasn't up for cleaning any of it out yet. After all, two years really wasn't that long. It had gone by so fast!

He hung up the towel, sprayed himself with Lydia's favorite lemongrass eucalyptus after-shower oil, and then walked naked into the bedroom. Venom followed closely behind again.

In the walk-in closet hung his pajamas, and he grabbed a set. Pulling it over his head, he smelled the air in the closet and caught her scent. Her clothes were still perfectly hung, categorized by color. Her shoes lined up in two rows underneath the clothes. She had scarves and belts and other things in opaque boxes with lids. She had leftover towels and sheets she arranged for both of them to use.

But even though one wall of the three-sided closet was Harper's, he still felt like it was Lydia's sanctuary. He turned out the light and walked over to the bed and crawled in on Lydia's side. He was careful not to step on or move her slippers, which sat by the bed side-by-side, ready for her tender feet and red-painted toenails.

Everything in this house waited for Lydia to come back.

And even though it smelled like she was here still,

as he buried his head in the pillowcase he had never washed and never would, he fell asleep dreaming about what it would feel like to have her legs wrapped around his, to have his arms tightly holding her body. His hands, scarred and bruised from all the missions he'd done, still faintly smelling like cordite, would be healed by rubbing up-and-down her spine from the top of her gorgeous derrière all the way to the back of her neck.

She was there with him, resting against him, on top of him, curled up inside his soul.

As if lending appreciation for his memories, Venom scooted closer to Harper, his body extending the full length of his. At the last minute, the dog placed his head very gently on Harper's chest.

This was his favorite thing about being home. Remembering Lydia. Loving her still. And letting Venom take care of him.

CHAPTER 4

"HOW THE HELL do you get out of Coronado so fast, Harper? I turned around and you were gone, disappeared. Hope everything's okay," Kyle told him over the phone.

The morning dew had just broken. Harper was researching on his computer out on the back deck, drinking his third cup of coffee. So much for serenity and being calm. And of course, calls from Kyle always jumbled him up a bit too.

"My dad's not doing so well up here. But you know how it is, people panic a little bit. I get here, and it's not quite so bad," he lied.

"Well, good, because I've got some terrible news for you."

"Not sure I want to hear it, Kyle. Can you call me back in about three hours?"

Before Kyle could utter something nasty, Harper interrupted the silence.

"Just kidding. Go ahead. Shoot, Kyle."

"I was going to say—but thank God you're all together.

"You making me wait for it?"

"Hang on. We've come across some intel, and it looks like the shooter you got—you know, the one we put down in Africa almost eighteen months ago now, the guy who got to Lydia?"

Harper sucked in air and barely got out, "Oh shit, no." He felt his blood pressure rise, and the vein on the right side of his neck begin to pulse like maybe it was going to really burst this time.

"Yeah, that guy. Turns out, we got the wrong intel. He was a shooter, and he was part of their squad, that Jakob Freedom militia from Benin. He definitely was a bad dude, but he wasn't *the* bad dude. And State Department thinks they have a way to get the actual guy this time. I just wanted to let you know you might be getting a call. And when you do, I want you to talk to me first before you give any answer to their questions. They're thinking about putting together a task force, multi-department sort of thing. And nobody knows about it in an official capacity, so you didn't hear it from me. I'm just giving you a heads-up so you can be prepared, that's all."

"This the part where I'm supposed to thank you or something. You wait until I get back home to tell me this?"

"Like I said, I tried."

"What do you mean by multi-department? You mean like a Special Forces group?"

"Yeah. That's what it is. Now you and I know, we can only listen to these things once or twice, and then we want to sit down and see the particulars, right? I mean they talk a good game, but when it comes right down to it, we're the ones who have to evaluate whether or not it's a good idea or whether or not we want to participate. My fear is, Harper—and this is just man-to-man because I love you, Brother, and I don't want to lose you—they're trying to pull you out of my team and put you in somebody else's."

"You mean somebody who's already set on a rotation to go out there quicker. Are you talking Africa then?"

"I'm not sure, because it's not Team 5. I called Hughes right away, and he's not heard a thing. So that tells me it might be somewhere else. Maybe Middle East, maybe Europe. I don't know."

"So you're saying the shooter is alive?"

"The one that actually did the assassination, yes. He is an Italian national. A revolutionary ever since he was like twelve years old. His parents were professors, educated in Russia and up to no good. He even did a stint here in the States as a minor traveling with his parents when they were teaching radical European history at Duncan University. I don't know where the parents are, but the kid grew up bent as hell, and he apparently joined this militia group thinking he could make a difference."

That stung. "Oh, he made a difference all right. Fuckin' asshole doesn't deserve to be alive."

"No argument with me on that, Harper. Anyway, turns out he's not quite in it for the violence. He likes being a little cushier. It was supposed to be a tryout, and he didn't pass. But he got lucky with a shot, Harper. Just one shot. Wasn't even aiming for her, but he got her anyway."

Now Harper was really pissed.

"And from what I understand, and Karin backs me up on this, he's putting together a group in Europe to do some possible large-scale bombings or terror campaigns, with help from funding by our enemies. Russia has a hand in it for sure. He supposedly doesn't want to work with the Africans anymore."

"While I hate the guy, I can certainly understand that. I think, in his shoes, I'd probably choose the same. So they're thinking of taking him down outside Africa?"

"Look, Harper, the less you know the better it's going to be, because you're one hell of a bad liar, and they'll see right through it if you know too much.

Besides, my information could be wrong. But I want you to talk to me before you decide anything, okay? They reached out to me for how to get a hold of you, and they want you to come back to D.C. and sit for an interview. I'm not sure it's something you have to do. I'm telling you as your LPO, because I really don't want to lose you, especially for some kind of an op that isn't under our complete control. You and I know not all the teams are the same. But my understanding is this would not be run by SEALs at all. Maybe civilian-run, and that makes me nervous."

"That doesn't make any sense. But okay, it's a deal. I'll talk to you about it before I decide to do anything. I'm not likely to jump in, but it sure would be nice to get rid of the guy. Maybe then some of my nightmares would stop."

Harper was older now. If he'd been in his twenties, he would've jumped at the chance to take down the guy, even if it cost him an arm, leg, eye, or his life. He wanted revenge and often made those types of decisions early on. But now, he had more to live for. He wanted to be careful, strategize. If he could do both things at once, well, then he might be interested. But he told Kyle not to worry and that as soon as he heard from the powers that be, he'd get back with him right away.

Harper surveyed the garden and the canyon below.

At the top of the swale on the other side, the pine trees were bright green at their tips, indicating they'd recently gone through a growth spurt. Everything was lush and green as it could be. Lydia would have loved the flower garden he created, which was twice the size of the one she saw when she was alive.

Venom was happy, resting at his feet. He could even see himself maybe doing some evening yoga events. It wasn't a great idea, but he was willing to suspend his negativity and consider it.

He dialed Hamish next.

"Hey there, are you about ready to leave?" Harper asked when his friend picked up on the first ring.

"Next week, my man. We're going right back into the vipers' den. Although, this time they know we're coming thanks to you assholes. You guys woke them up real good."

"I got it. And look, I'm sorry."

"I know you didn't call me just to say goodbye. That would be stupid as hell, so everything okay at home?"

"I'm having some trouble with my dad, but he's strong as an ox. It's just his brain is letting him down. Gotta see if we can change his meds or do something, because right now, they want to tie him up and throw him in a padded cell."

"Jesus Christ. Something like that happens to me,

Harper, promise me you'll just give me a nice bullet to the brain, okay?"

"Same here, Buddy. But you know how Dad is. I can't do that to him. I just have to find a way to help. I'm not sure what that means yet."

"Okay, so it's not about saying goodbye, and it's not about talking about your dad. What's the real reason you're calling? Otherwise, I have to go, because my wife is walking around in her underwear. You know that only lasts for a little while, and then she starts putting clothes on. When she gets her running shoes on, well, then it's too late, if you know what I mean? Let's hurry this up."

"I gotcha." Harper knew it was the right thing to call Hamish. "It looks like the guy who did Lydia is still out there. Now you didn't hear this from me—"

"Fuck me. How did they screw that up? You hit that son of a bitch right in the middle of his forehead. I saw the fuckin' pictures. That dude was dead. You mean to tell me he lived?"

"Yes, he lived. Because we hit the wrong guy."

"Okay, that changes things a little bit. But aren't they going to put a team together to go after him? And that would be something we would certainly do for you. Why would they call you? Unless they want you to try to attach to our team. You think about joining Team 5, Harper?"

"No, Sir. I like where I'm at. It would be something else, like a TDA. And you can't breathe a word of this to anybody."

"Understood. No worries there."

"But I still got to ask you, do you think that's something I should consider if they give me an opportunity to insert, take a small team with me, and go after this guy? I mean, I don't even know if it's really going to happen, but I have it on good authority—"

"Which means Kyle called you, right?"

"I'm not saying, but that is a good guess, Hamish. I want to hear you talk to me about this. And, Hamish, I want you to try to talk me out of it."

"Oh, that's a stupid idea. You want to off the guy, right? Why couldn't they just keep an eye on him, track him, and then when you guys are back in rotation in six months, you guys can get all biblical on him. And he'll wish he was dead before you get there. That's how it should happen. What's the emergency?

"I'm wondering the same thing, so I guess there are more details I'm going to find out about. Help me with the questions."

"It doesn't sound like anything we don't do every day, Harper. You're saying they're going to call you and not go through the Navy or your liaison or Kyle?"

"Okay, that's the first question. Yeah, I want to ask that. What else would you want to know?"

Hamish gave a big sigh, sounding halfway annoyed. "Well, I guess it all depends on where he is. Is he going through a location that'll be easier to get him now than later? Depends on where he hangs out. If you tell me he's a Russian or Ukrainian or former KGB agent, I'm not going to commit to any kind of behind-the-Russian-border thing. Maybe that's what they're talking about. Maybe it wasn't an African after all. Guess you just need more information, like who he is and where he is living and why the urgency."

"Fair enough. Okay. Anything else?"

"I might have some other ideas. Right now, just to be honest with you because you're my very best friend, I need to get close and naked with my lady. And there ain't nothing in the world as important as that. So you hang on, and maybe in about five hours I'll be ready to talk to you. Okay?"

Harper laughed. "You're an asshole, Hamish. But you're my kind of asshole. Have a good time."

"I intend to. No doubt about it." Hamish hung up before Harper could shoot back something smart and disrespectful.

Venom alerted to something going on up on the hillside. It was outside of his fence line, but something definitely was making its way through the forest. Harper could hear the sounds of twigs and small branches breaking. It was possible it was a pack of coyotes or maybe one very big boar. But there was something out there, something Venom sensed was an enemy.

He leaned over and patted the dog's head. "What did you see out there, Venom? What is it?"

Venom scrambled to his feet and nearly pointed in the direction of where he heard the noise. They both listened carefully. Again, there was a rustling of leaves and brush. A flock of quail flew up into the sky, having been spooked by some animal or a man.

Harper went inside the kitchen, and leaning next to the back door on the inside was his rifle with a high-powered scope on it. He got it out, and from the shadows inside the house, he looked through to see if he could discover a form, especially a human form. Finally, he zeroed in on a thick clump of branches moving. As Venom jumped off the deck and ran down into the canyon to head up the hill to the fence line, Harper saw what it was.

She was the largest mountain lion Harper had ever seen in this part of the county. She was wrestling a small deer to the ground, and when she looked up, the deer still struggling in front of her, her face was bloodied from her nose all the way up to her ears on her left side. At her feet were two small cubs.

He watched Venom run up to the fence line, barking and jumping as if he could scale over all ten feet plus the barbed wire casing on top. The mountain lion studied him as the cubs sat, fully alert and facing the house. Venom was barking uncontrollably. Through the scope, Harper could see she was bending to yank the carcass one or two more times to end the life of the small deer and then begin to drag it away with the little cubs in tow.

"That's a good mama, providing for your babies. That'll keep them fat and healthy for a week. I'm not going to mess with you, Sweetheart. You're just doing the right thing," he whispered.

He sat his rifle back down, leaning it against the door frame, came out to the back deck, and whistled for Venom to return. Dutifully, he didn't stop barking, but he turned around and ran back in Harper's direction, stopping every few yards to jump, turn around, and face the mountain lion's position before continuing on his path toward Harper.

"That's a good boy, Venom. It was just mountain lions, a nice healthy female and her cubs. She's just doing what she's supposed to do. And hell, Venom, we got so much deer around here she could take one a day and we still wouldn't be depleted. Those cubs deserve a good start and lots of fresh meat. She's a good mother. You leave her alone, okay?"

Harper swore the dog knew exactly what he'd just told him.

He returned to his online studies—a new research on dementia and treatment for early onset dementia, all the stages and signs, medicines, and therapies that might slow the process. But just as he knew from his previous research, there was no cure for it. It was a losing battle.

About four o'clock in the afternoon, he got a call from Washington, D.C.. It was Admiral Patterson, a member of the Joint Chiefs.

"SO Cunningham, I am pleased to make your acquaintance, and unfortunately, I've not met you in person."

"Honored, Sir. Please call me Harper. What can I do for you?"

"Very well. I'll get right to it without the small talk, if you don't mind."

"Fine by me, Sir."

"We are considering a special team, a special team of operators from several branches of the military and other assets as well. All U.S., no foreign assets. I'd like to discuss it with you, and I'm going to send a transport to Santa Rosa to pick you up tomorrow. I'd like you to come for a visit, so I can sit down and talk to you about what we have in mind."

"What has facilitated this, Admiral, if you don't mind my asking? I'm extremely flattered, but I'm just a little guy here. I'm not an officer or team leader. I'm just a grunt. Why call me?"

"Because the individual we want you to hunt down and bring back is the individual we believe was responsible for your wife's assassination. We thought you would be the perfect person to head up this new team."

"Until today, I understood that sonofabitch had already been returned to the Source."

"This turned out to be inaccurate information. A man was returned, but not the one responsible."

"You have proof of this?" he asked Patterson.

"We do. And you shall see it."

Harper hesitated. "But I don't do commands. I don't want to be in charge of anybody. I can barely be in charge of myself."

"My wife says the same of me. So I understand. But we think you're uniquely qualified, and we know you have the proper motivation to make this work for us. The President of the United States has asked me to contact you personally. He will also be sitting in on the meeting."

Harper was at a loss for words. His heart was ready to run down into the woods and chase after that mountain lion. His gut told him this meeting would change his life, and he suspected not in a good way. He didn't trust anyone above Kyle's rank, no matter who they were.

"Harper, tomorrow's the only day we can do this.

The president doesn't usually get no for an answer. I'd like your commitment that you'll be on that plane when it arrives tomorrow at ten o'clock."

CHAPTER 5

H ARPER WAS EDGY all afternoon after the call with
the admiral. He packed, bringing just enough for
a two-day stay. He'd wear a sports jacket and his
polished loafers on the plane, so everything else was
light and would fit in one duffel bag.

He had permission to wear his sidearm and
brought along a journal for notes, sticking it in his
laptop case he'd carry over his shoulder. He didn't
want anyone rummaging through any checked baggage
when he flew commercial, so he was accustomed to
traveling this way.

He let Venom outside to wander a bit while he
watched over him. The sun tilted toward the west and
would set in just shy of two hours. That gave him an
idea.

He put on his long running pants, running shoes, a
t-shirt, and a lightweight parka. Then he grabbed
Venom, and the two of them headed toward the coast,

which would take them nearly thirty minutes.

He'd used the seat warmers so that by the time he pulled into the parking lot at Goat Rock State Beach, even through the thick fleece he pulled from the second seat, the driver's side would stay warm and toasty for Venom. The truck was angled closest to the ocean, with a perfect view of the beach and the gathering of yoga enthusiasts below.

"I'll be about an hour, Venom. You stay put and watch." He showed the dog the bowl of water he'd placed on the passenger side floor for him.

Then he cracked the windows and locked the doors all around.

He'd brought an old blanket tucked under one arm as he made it down the narrow trail that led to the shore. Several people had gathered already, staking out their places. Harper spread the blanket at the outside of the group, midway back.

The instructor was facing the west in a resting meditation pose, legs crossed, palms upturned and resting on her bent knees, her thumb and third finger touching on both hands. As he sat and stretched to touch his toes, which was difficult for him, she abruptly stood up and addressed the group.

Harper turned to check on Venom and saw his companion stoically sitting tall in the driver seat, inspecting every move in front of him.

Her name was Evie, and the photograph on her brochure was nice but didn't do her justice in the flesh. Her long blonde hair was tied in a braid that hung midway down her back. She wore a one-piece aqua-blue bodysuit that showed every curve in her supple, lithe body. With graceful arms extended to the sides, she encouraged everyone to stand and do the same.

Harper shed his parka and followed suit.

She led the group in several stretches, toe-touches, back bends, arches, and waist turns and tilts. They pressed against their elbows as they wrapped themselves first in one arm and then the other. They did lunges and then Warrior Pose several times, Harper having trouble with his balance.

She asked them to be seated, where they began floor stretches.

He wasn't as flexible as most of the other participants. His muscle mass was easily twice the size of anyone else's, but he forced himself as far as he could. Some wrapped themselves into pretzel-like forms, which were impossible for him to do. It surprised him when Evie came over to him and gently guided his frame into modified positions that enabled him to do the stretch or pose she was instructing. The touch of her fingers against his body gave him the shivers.

It had been a long time since he'd felt a woman's touch. Was he that starved for attention? Some of his body parts started to respond in spite of the screaming going on inside his head to demand they stop.

Harper would have preferred to run back and forth on the beach like he was used to doing, with fifty or sixty pounds of rocks in his rucksack, wearing ankle-high steel-toed combat boots. That would have been no problem. But holding his breath, leaning, and stretching toward the bright orange sky while keeping his balance was impossible. He fell several times.

Once again, she came over, as she did for others, and adjusted his body so that he was more comfortable, and each time she touched him, he felt his groin lurch. It was damned annoying. This went on for nearly an hour. He was going to leave early after struggling with the poses the entire time, until she announced the last pose before cool down. He was almost there! He'd almost made it through his first yoga class!

The cow-cat movement of dumping and arching his torso while on all fours like a cow or a cat seemed simple enough until she added the quick breath exercises, breathing in during the cow and breathing out during the cat pose. And then they sped up. It was hard not to think about having sex. The sounds of the ocean, the breathing in and out, the little moans people made while doing so threw him into a trance. All at once, he was having sex with Lydia, pumping her hard and working to make her explode.

He started ejaculating uncontrollably so threw himself on the blanket, trying to hide it. He felt like a school kid reacting to a forbidden nude photo. Filled with shame and embarrassment, he felt like he'd cheated on Lydia, which didn't make any sense at all!

Someone snickered. He would have left, but that would have drawn too much attention to the huge wet patch in his crotch. Were he by himself, he'd immediately dive into the cool surf and then wrap in the blanket, but he didn't and suffered instead. He diverted his gaze from Evie, who showed him with that sultry stare and half-smile that she knew. Oh yes, she knew.

He was completely mortified. This had been such a mistake.

She continued with the cool down, which helped quell his libido and bring him back to sanity. The slow breathing in and out calmed his nerves as he cleared his head and brought himself back to some sense of peace in his inner sanctum. And then it was all over.

Finally!

Evie invited people to stay who wanted to sit and enjoy the violent orange sunset before returning home. That appealed to Harper, who feigned being too cold and wrapped the blanket around himself, hiding his wet pants from anyone who would dare look his way.

He'd spent many hours at the beach both before

and after Lydia, and the sunsets never ceased to amaze him. The power of the cloud-riddled sky hovering over the ocean, blanketing it with a reflection of the warm, dying sun were breathtaking tonight. Stars began to poke out of the deep turquoise blue-turning-navy-heavens. The clouds turned grey and then faded into the dark sky, and soon, even the orange glow at the horizon was lost to the night.

He hadn't noticed that nearly everyone had left already. He heard engines starting and car doors slamming, which brought his attention to the here and now. He stood, wrapping himself again in the blanket as Evie came over to him.

"Are you a friend of Sally's?" she asked.

"How did you know?"

"She is great at descriptions. Judging from the size of your shoulders and the full sleeves, I figured you might be."

"Oh, these?" he said, extending his right arm graced with numerous tribal rings he'd picked up after every deployment. He also bore the frog prints many of the men on SEAL Team 3 had inked onto their forearms and into their souls.

"Quite impressive." She smiled.

"I'm afraid I'm lousy at this."

"Be patient. It's a practice, takes time. You'll get it, and in the meantime, it will teach you patience. You'll see. Trust me."

He wanted to. That's when he realized he wasn't good at talking to women, either. In fact, he felt awkward standing in front of her under the stars, having any kind of conversation at all. He didn't belong here.

When he didn't respond, she continued. "I commend you for even trying. Yoga teaches you mental strength so that your body doesn't have to be a vessel of armor. It can become flexible, soft, but still strong. It does teach you to relax."

Was she coming on to him? It wasn't what he wanted.

She stepped closer to him so that he could feel her body heat.

"No," he said as he stepped back, leaving a good two feet between them.

"But Sally said—"

"Well, Sally shouldn't pretend to know me. This wasn't why I came."

"I completely understand your hesitation. I just thought—"

"Hesitation? I have no hesitation! It's a *choice*. Come to think of it, not a very good one either."

He re-tightened his blanket around his torso, making sure all the evidence of his shameful transgression was hidden, and began to walk off.

"Thank you," she shouted to his back. "I hope you come back another time."

Frustrated and mumbling to himself, kicking himself in the ass for his complete stupidity and lack of judgment, he chalked it up to the nerves he was carrying around, worrying about his meeting tomorrow. Who the heck did she think she was? He was going to be meeting the President of the United States, and he might have to tell the man that no, he wasn't interested. Whatever they were going to offer him, he wasn't interested.

Opening the driver door, Venom adjusted to move over and sit in the passenger seat like he had on the way over. Harper carefully scooped himself onto the seat, still partially covered by the blanket, perching on top of the warm fleece. He was careful to keep his seat clean.

When he glanced at Venom, he saw the dog had been staring at his crotch and then met him eyeball-to-eyeball.

"Not you too, Venom. Don't start with me. It was an accident."

As if he understood, Venom turned and faced the windshield as Harper drove the two of them away to safety.

CHAPTER 6

HARPER WAS MET at Dulles International Airport by Admiral Patterson's driver, dressed in civilian clothes, which made Harper nervous as hell. The kid didn't look older than high school age, but Harper was used to feeling old, especially these past couple of years. He couldn't tell an eighteen-year-old from a mid-twenties tadpole.

"Nolan Pierce. Welcome to Washington," the kid said as he extended his hand.

"Harper Cunningham. Please call me Harper." He kept the handshake as brief as possible.

"You have luggage?" the young driver asked.

"Just this." He held up his duffel and turned to the side so Pierce could see his computer case. "And I am armed. I'm required to divulge this to you, just so you know."

"I will inform the admiral of this, of course. He's waiting for you outside."

Harper was led through the bustling airport lobby, full of groups of tourists and business men and women racing to catch flights to and from all over the world. He could count on one hand the number of times he'd been here, and always, it was for some kind of a ceremonial function. He had been the honor guard for several team members he'd been close to who didn't make it home.

But today was completely different. The Suburban at the arrival and pickup area was allowed to idle, unlike the general population. The windows were blacked out. Local airport police ignored the vehicle, which sported the special starred D.C. plates indicative of the passenger's rank. Pierce opened the rear door and spoke to the admiral quietly, then nodded, backed up, and made room for Harper to gain entry.

The two men sat alone in the rear.

Admiral Patterson shook his hand. "I'm glad you could make it, SO Cunningham."

"Harper. It's Harper, sir. I don't want to hear SO anything, if you don't mind."

Admiral Patterson leaned forward, putting his hand on the driver's shoulder.

"Nolan, we have to make good time here. I'd like not to have the president wait too long."

"I understand, Sir. I'll do the very best I can. We'll get you there on time," Pierce answered.

The admiral turned to Harper. "Are you comfortable? Want some water or something stronger perhaps?"

"No, thanks, Admiral. I'm good. I do have some questions, if you don't mind?"

"Go right ahead. Nolan here has clearance, but he wears ear buds."

"Thank you. You said you had some proof about the misinformation."

Harper figured it might as well be something they talk about right away since, if there was some kind of an error made, he didn't want to be airing dirty laundry in front of the commander-in-chief.

"Yes. Turns out that this particular person—his name was Commander or General Okubo, you'll recall—was originally the one taking credit for murdering several of the missionaries that day. It was assumed Lydia was among them. I think in the fog of war, the statements from survivors were found not to be accurate. It took us awhile to get the proper DNA testing, and her DNA was initially not found. However, I do have a photograph, and this picture is rather graphic. I must ask your permission first before I show it to you."

"A picture of Lydia?" Harper's mouth went completely dry. He coughed into his hand.

"We wanted confirmation, if you could. But are

you sure?"

Harper sucked in air and nodded, preparing himself for something he never expected nor wanted to see.

"This was taken by one of the aid workers. There was a trial in Benin, and this was offered into evidence that Okubo was the perpetrator. Except it was determined that it wasn't him."

The admiral handed Harper the top photograph, holding several others on his lap.

"You can clearly see this gentleman standing over a woman's body. Is this Lydia?"

Harper held the picture. Lydia's chest was red with blood, a stain nearly as wide as her tiny body. Otherwise, the grainy photograph revealed very little. He was sure it was her. The man standing nearby was not Okubo.

His voice broke as he uttered, "That's not the shooter I nailed. This guy is smaller. That's not Okubo."

"This is Lydia then?"

"Yes, Admiral." Harper felt wetness well up in his eyes. His stomach growled, and briefly, he thought he was going to be sick all over the back seat. He box breathed several rotations, and the dark spots in his eyes faded while the sickness in his stomach subsided.

Admiral Patterson handed over another three pictures, taken at intervals, showing the shooter bending over Lydia, picking her lifeless body up—her head rolling back, arms and legs dangling—and putting her in the back of a truck bed with several other bodies.

The admiral whispered, "We understand all the bodies were taken to a burn pit and destroyed. That's why the DNA was so messed up. We couldn't find everybody, and initially, her DNA was not obtained. Later, it showed up. I'm so sorry."

Harper's eyes were red and hot, without the tears he knew he'd shed tonight in the shower. He was hoping that was the end of the photographs, but no, the admiral still had a wad of them left.

"Who is this guy, then?" Harper asked. "You have more pictures there?"

"Not of him. These are some of the others. I brought them in case you wanted to see. Those are the only ones of Lydia. I'm so sorry, Son."

"I never got any of this information before we went over. So I killed a bad guy, just not the bad guy I thought I was getting. That's what you're saying, right? And now you want me to go in and complete this job? Am I saying this right?"

"Yes. Until he surfaced in Italy, we were not going to make this information available to anybody. It was a new, separate piece of intel about him. It came up during the trial of some of Okubo's surviving militia. Until then, we had no idea he even existed. We assumed the Africans did it. But clearly this guy isn't one of them."

Son of a bitch, Harper thought to himself. Just like military. Not denying information, yet camouflaging mistakes and nefarious activities. Covering up things to sanitize them. It was why he didn't even like hanging around any of the senior officers, anyone from the head shed. He'd been told one tale too many over the years. A bunch of amateurs. He knew it was common to get rid of bad operators by promoting them up when they deserved to be kicked out.

"I'm in awe of your background and service to this country, Harper. I've read your file. You've passed up advancements, stopped even trying to get promoted. Is there a reason why?"

"I don't want to do it. I don't want to lead. I want to follow."

"And why is that? Wouldn't you have more control if you were in charge?"

He was right, of course. All the things he hated about the military involved having to work for somebody he didn't respect or didn't trust. And there had been a lot of bad information, intel that cost lives. That's why he was on Kyle's team. He was the most respected LPO on the West Coast Teams, to his own peril. Kyle really went out of his way to protect his guys. Anyone on SEAL Team 3 felt themselves lucky to be under his charge.

"It's a long story, Sir. I just try to stick to what I'm good at. I like long-term relationships with my military leaders. I like working with people I trust. I'm not sure how I would feel taking orders from somebody I've never met, orders over a phone in the middle of some kind of an insurrection, coup, or militia takeover. I just don't like the set up."

"Independent, aren't you?" asked Patterson.

"Nah, I'd say stupidly stubborn. But that isn't going to change, Sir. I hope you're not counting on that."

Patterson nodded. "I completely understand."

"Who was this guy in the photograph?"

"Jakob Lipori. He's an Italian national and, as far as we know, never went back to Africa, but he definitely was there. He worked with Okubo for a few weeks."

They were ushered around the back side of the White House, where he was stopped and registered, given a visitor badge, and required to surrender his sidearm. They picked up an escort and were brought to the second floor, waiting in a small foyer as aides and White House staff zoomed by quickly, in and out of doorways, carrying paperwork, whispering plans or agendas. None of these people paid them any attention.

The two waited approximately an hour, and finally, a young staffer showed them into another anteroom leading to the Oval Office.

Now Harper's hands began to sweat. "You have any tips for me?" he asked the admiral.

"You're right to feel nervous. President Collins is a fine man. He's not afraid. Sometimes, I think his combat experience is missing from his life now that he's stuck behind a desk. He was an early UDT guy, you know."

"Yes, I understood that."

"He never talks about it much. I respect that. No stolen valor with him. I think he fancies himself still engaged in enemy combat. He'll like you, I'm sure. He's also very stubborn and independent. Just tell the truth and answer curtly."

This was not going be difficult for Harper to do. He hated long explanations and people who waxed eloquent over bullshit.

A few minutes later, they were escorted into the Oval Office and introduced. The president was sitting on a loveseat across a coffee table from an identical loveseat and stood as soon as they made their way inside.

President Collins shook his hand with firm resolve. *Just like a SEAL,* Harper thought. Having gotten that part of the pissing contest out of the way, he studied the president's face. He liked that the man looked him straight in the eyes.

"I'm very pleased to meet you, Special Operator

Cunningham," he said. "I've heard a lot about you, and I am so sorry for the loss of your wife. I understand she was a very gifted nurse, and you had attempted to travel with her, but your team was delayed. I'm sorry about that, and I hope you will bear with us while we propose something you might be interested in. I hope you'll be interested in it anyway."

Harper had been stuck on the inaccuracy, which annoyed him. "Actually, Sir, that's not quite accurate. Her timing was bumped up. Our deployment was set in stone. But she had to go ahead. I tried to talk her out of it, but she just wouldn't hear of it. I want to make sure that nothing negatively reflects on SEAL Team 3 or my LPO, Kyle Lansdowne. Because that wouldn't be fair."

"Yes, I've heard of Chief Lansdowne. He's an invaluable resource to the Teams. Legendary, you could say."

"Indeed. They don't make many like him. That's why I haven't retired. I frankly don't know what else I would do." Harper wondered if that was the right thing to say under the circumstances.

The president pointed to the seat across from him, asking them to sit. He did the same and crossed his legs. "What have you heard about this mission?"

Harper looked at Admiral Patterson and then back at the president. "Sir, Mr. President, I'm sorry, but I've not been told much except that you are looking to put together a team to go after the real shooter. And I've seen a couple photographs. Honestly, those are photographs I never wanted to see. But I understand. I don't know what it is I can do, so I just thought I'd hear you out and then I'll let you know what I think. It sounds like you're putting together some kind of a group. And you want me to consider joining that group. I have lots of questions and concerns about it."

"I imagine you do. Let me put it to you briefly. We have a whole write up, a prospectus on what we're trying to organize here, but in a nutshell, we would like to recruit several senior members from different branches of the military, CIA, and State operatives, people who are still active in the field but of advanced years and possibly considering retirement. I don't think forty-five years of age is advanced. You're a youngster to me, still in your prime."

Harper knew that when the compliments started flying so did the bullshit. He was ready for it.

"But many, especially the operators on the Teams, are done by the time they hit thirty-five. You're an anomaly, Harper. We don't want to lose our senior members with some of the best experience. Maybe the HALO jumps or difficult missions in Africa, Middle East, other places are starting to get old and lose their luster. It's one thing to do those missions when you're in your twenties. Many of those guys don't have families yet. You have to admit, some of this is for younger men. But your experience as a nearly twenty-year operator outweighs the challenges of your age. I'm aware of the fact that many of you have to have hip replacements or knee replacements well before you're forty due to all the jumps and trainings you go through. It takes a toll on one's body."

Harper listened, but he stared at the president's shoes and socks. He had placed two different socks on his feet. Harper wondered why no staffer had pointed it out to him.

"That's true, Mr. President. I've complained about my body quite a bit. But we just get it done anyway. You learn how to do things without getting hurt. So while I may be older than some of the newer guys, I still qualify expert every test we have, and I'm one of the fastest runners. So why not just tell me what you have in mind?"

Patterson leaned forward and added to the president's information.

"Son, we would like to start a new SEAL Team, and for lack of a better description, we're going to call it Silver Team. We have to get authorization before we can formally put it to work, but prior to that, we would like to use a group of you on an experimental basis to stop what we believe is a terrorist cell growing in

Europe. We'd like to see how it works out, and this would mean a deployment to Italy."

"But that's what the Teams do now," Harper objected.

The admiral nodded. "Depending on the country, yes. However, there may be cases where we don't have agreements of State. We're going to need to gingerly go around those rules somehow, and I guess what the president is saying is we want to do this on a trial basis. We want to stop this terrorist cell and get to his new recruits before they go into action."

President Collins interrupted. "We want to see if, with your unique experience, you could lead the team to go in, grab the sniper, and get out before anyone knows you're there, just like the Teams do. He lives in a village outside of Florence when he's not working elsewhere in Europe. He's posing as a farmer and successful Italian businessman. He grows olives and makes olive oil, but that's his cover. In fact, he has recruited and trained other European revolutionary types. Young kids from the Universities. He stays away from Africans and Middle Eastern militia types."

"He works alone? Not part of a network?" Harper asked.

"He's creating a network. Apparently, he was in Africa at the raid—the militia raid on the health clinic that Lydia was at, but he did not appreciate working with or for the militia leader and, after the raid, went back to Italy. We think he's vulnerable because he doesn't know we know who he is and what he's done or what he's in the process of doing. The intel we have is extremely accurate, and it's a snatch and grab. But it also could be a capture-and-kill mission. That's why I can't have anybody running this team other than a SEAL. And I want someone who's experienced and motivated. I think you fit that bill."

CHAPTER 7

H ARPER RETURNED TO the rear entrance of the
White House with the admiral. Tucked under his
arm was the thick prospectus of the new Silver Team.

"You're sure you don't want to spend the night in
Washington? We can put you up at the Four Seasons.
It's a beautiful hotel, recently refurbished. That way, if
you like, you can have a further discussion with the
president tomorrow. Depending on when, I will try to
fit you in." The admiral was visibly shaken that Harper
had not accepted President Collins' invitation to join.

"I have to get back. I've got a father suffering from
dementia, and I promised I would get back to some of
my teammates in San Diego on the way home. If
possible, I'd like to be flown back there tonight. From
San Diego, I'll catch a plane to Santa Rosa on my dime.
But I need to speak with my LPO and one of my
friends. I'll crash there overnight."

"I understand. And as you requested, inside the

prospectus is a list of names we'd like you to consider giving your evaluation, if you know these gentlemen. One of them on the list is your LPO, Kyle Lansdowne. Wouldn't it be to your advantage to work with him again?"

"Well, that's assuming he would accept this job. Has he?"

"No, I believe he has not. I am not sure if the president has even informed him. We frankly thought you would be accepting the position, since the income is so generous. It's double what you were making on the Teams. You'd be working with the best of the best, since safety is always a concern. We honestly hadn't thought of a Plan B."

As the vehicle was brought around the back, Harper turned in his badge, retrieved his favorite Sig, and stood outside the open rear door.

"It's just the way I do things, Admiral. And I need to make sure it wouldn't impact my father's situation at the Veterans care facility. I still like to sleep on it in my own bed first before I make any important decision."

"Understood."

"If you like, I won't mention the names to my LPO, but I would prefer discussing it with him and showing him the prospectus. As far as anybody else on your list, I haven't glanced at it, so I have no idea who you've got there. But I would like to discuss this with Kyle since he is my current boss. Only being respectful of our chain of command."

"That's acceptable to us, Harper. How much time do you need?"

"I'd say give me a week."

"A week?" His eyes squinted, and the edges of his mouth rolled down, clearly negatively affected by Harper's answer. "I'm sure I don't have to tell you that time is of the essence. As you know, these types of individuals move around a lot, and while we don't have a current actionable terrorist plot, these things do pop up rather quickly, and I would hate the delay. I wouldn't want to cause any loss of property or life. We're not trying to force you into something; we're just trying to avoid some kind of an international incident, if we can."

"Understood. I promise I will get back to you either way. In the meantime, feel free to text or call me. We don't have to be out of touch. If I have further questions, I will go through you. If in my discussions with Kyle he comes up with some questions, would you mind if we talk to you jointly?"

"Of course. Feel free."

"So unless I can't get a plane out tonight, I'd like to be taken back to the airport and put on the next flight to Coronado."

While Admiral Patterson worked the details, Pierce

raced back to Dulles Airport, just in time for him to catch a connecting flight with a layover of several hours in Houston. It wasn't Harper's favorite spot, but he wanted to get out of D.C. as quickly as possible. With a special Club Card, he had use of the phones and the facilities there—even a room for taking a nap or a shower if he needed it. He didn't feel like hanging out in the terminal any longer than he needed to. He took the flight to Houston then walked through the automatic glass doors of the Club and waited in a short line to register.

Checking his ticket, he noted he was going to land by 0100. He'd book his return home to Santa Rosa when he was done, but he needed to let Sally know, since she was watching Venom for him again. He checked in and decided to give her a call with a possible ETA.

"Delayed again? You're not going to make me wait up for you this time?"

"I'll make sure not to. I only need a day in San Diego, and I'll text you when I make the return flight reservations. Once I know, you can bring him over to wait at my place, if you want."

"Well, that would depend on when you get in." She sounded annoyed.

"That's fine. If he gets restless, just bring him up to my house and let him in. And text me so I know he's there by himself. I'll leave it up to you, Sally. And I'm so sorry for this inconvenience."

"I hope it was successful and important. You sure took off quickly. Must've been something last minute. I hope everything's okay, Harper."

"Oh, yes, I had an interesting conversation with some people I'll tell you about later. But again, Sally, I sure do appreciate you taking care of Venom and, of course, taking care of me."

"Just call me Mom. I'm old enough to be."

Harper chuckled. "And I never got to thank you before for getting me hooked up with Evie, the yoga teacher, but you probably ought to stop doing that. I don't seem to do well around women these days. And I'd really like not to have to play that game. But I appreciate your concern for me. I'm just not ready. She's beautiful, but she's just not my type. And I don't think anybody would be."

"I understand. And I'm sorry. She's very nice, but that's all I can say."

Next, Harper dialed Kyle, but all he got was Kyle's voicemail, so his message was brief and rather cryptic.

"I'll be back down there early this morning and was going to crash at Hamish's house. Maybe if you're up and free, we can grab some breakfast together. I got some things I need to show you about my meeting."

Next, he called Hamish.

"Well, this is going to be a record. I usually only talk to you once or twice a month. This is twice in the same week. Everything okay?" Hamish asked him.

"I have some things I need to discuss, and I'm going to be getting into Coronado early this morning, between one and two. Can I crash at your place or do you want me to catch a hotel near the airport?"

"You don't have a car? Where are you flying from?" Hamish asked.

"I'll get a cab to your house, and don't offer to pick me up. That's just too ridiculous. I took a last-minute trip to D.C. for an important meeting I want to tell you about."

"I'm going to have a hard time sleeping with all this intrigue. But, yeah, just come on in. I'll leave the back door open and pillows on the couch in the living room. I have no returnees this weekend."

Hamish used the term "returnees" to refer to his teenagers and older kids, who had a habit of coming home for the weekend and bringing several friends.

"And I'll see you in the morning. Are you sure everything's okay?"

"I think it is. But I have some decisions to make. I thought maybe you could help me with some of them."

"Okay, Man, see you later on. Safe travels."

With his back to windows overlooking the tarmac, in a corner where he could view the whole lounge easily and no one could sneak up behind him, he very gingerly opened the large portfolio book, tabbed and three-hole punched, scanned through the different topics, and found the list of names.

At the top of the list was Kyle Lansdowne's name. Right beneath it was Hamish's. He scanned the rest of the names and saw a few he recognized, some of the older guys from SEAL Team 3 and SEAL Team 5, a couple from Teams on the East Coast. He didn't recognize any of the CIA assets or State Department special agents. None of the bureaucrats either. It was a list that was quite long, which surprised him.

He slowly closed the notebook, tucking it into his computer case. Stowing the case in the leather lounge chair he was sitting in, with the duffel bag at his feet, he leaned back, closed his eyes, and found himself back in Africa. That day had been a hard trek in the jungle sun. He'd waited all afternoon in a treetop that held two huge ant colonies dangling down over three feet from a nearby branch. Harper had been very careful to pinch those little buggers off his flesh before he could get bitten, but it was getting annoying, and he was getting sleepy. If he fell asleep, he'd either fall out of the tree or get eaten alive by insects. So he waited. He pinched bugs and told a couple of jokes over the coms to Fredo and Armando.

And finally, when his patience was near at the end,

he heard over the coms that a Jeep was arriving and that Okubo was in it.

The six snipers who waited for his group were some of the best on SEAL Team 3. Harper had requested they allow him to take out Okubo. It was over in a matter of thirty seconds after they appeared in the clearing. Since there weren't any hostages located, they began firing immediately. Okubo had been spared the rest of the Team's rounds until Harper got a bead on him, inhaled, deliberately exhaled, and then pressed the hair trigger. He followed the trajectory in slow motion, although it took no more than a second to reach the middle of his forehead. The man's skull exploded into pieces all over the rest of the bodies in the sluggishly self-driving Jeep with a dead driver at the wheel.

He slipped his rifle to the side and examined the scene one more time. Then he checked it with his scope and confirmed that Okubo was indeed dead.

"He's done. Let's go home, Gents," he said into his Invisio.

Armando congratulated him on his perfect shot. "I hope you feel better, Harper. Glad this guy is off the face of the Earth."

"Yeah, we took care of business, Armando."

But inside, Harper had wondered why he didn't feel any better.

CHAPTER 8

HARPER PULLED UP to Hamish's house in a taxi, running around to the backside of the cozy house, and let himself in, locking the door behind him. He brought his duffel and briefcase into the living room, placing them next to the couch that was piled with clean pillows and a stack of fuzzy blankets. Slipping off his shoes, he next removed his sport coat, placed it over the back of a chair, tiptoed in his stocking feet to the kitchen, got himself a tall glass of water, and then quietly made it just in time to the guest bathroom for a long pee.

He returned to the living room and stripped off his button-down long-sleeved shirt, leaving his t-shirt on. Next, he removed his slacks and gently placed them over the back of another chair. At last, he tucked himself into the soft blankets on the couch quite comfortably. And as soon as his head hit the pillow, he was out.

Way too early in the morning, he heard conversations, and then he smelled bacon, followed by hearing a couple of girls giggling close by. Opening one eye at a time, he watched three cute little preteens, all three sporting braces, sitting cross-legged on the floor about ten feet away from him. Sasha, Hamish's youngest daughter, was right in the middle between her two friends.

"Hello, Uncle Harper," she said with coyness.

"Sasha! How long have you guys been down here?"

"Oh, about ten minutes, Uncle Harper. Why didn't you come earlier?"

"Well, that's what airplanes do. They have their own schedule. They put me on pretty late, so I got in past midnight. Did you hear me?"

She shook her head.

"Better to get in late than have to spend another day in the airport, right?"

She grinned, showing off her colored wire braces. They had rainbow colors done up in a unique and quite artful design.

"Is your dad still in bed upstairs?" he asked Sasha.

"I guess so. Do you want me to go check?"

"No, no, no, let's just let them sleep. Any chance I might be able to get a little more rest?"

"Oh, come on, Uncle Harper. We've got a soccer game today. Wouldn't you like to come watch us play?"

Harper knew Sasha had a huge girl crush on him, and he'd discussed it with Hamish, who didn't seem to mind, but he still warned Harper not to lead her on and break her heart—or his buddy would adjust his spine really good.

Ever since that discussion, Harper gently reminded Sasha she was way too young for him, but she still laughed it off every time he told her. "Now, if you were my age, I'd be very interested."

That seemed to do more for her ego than anything else he could've said.

"I smell bacon, ladies. Anyone want to cook me some breakfast?" he asked, scanning the three faces.

"Sure!" The shorter of the three, a little blonde girl in braids, got up, hiked her pajama bottoms, and dashed to the kitchen.

Harper lay back on the pillow, closing his eyes. He heard Sasha and her other friend get up and join their friend in the kitchen. The happy banter and light music coming from the kitchen was soothing. He fell asleep again, thinking Hamish was a very, very lucky man.

He was exhausted. He'd had four hours sleep, which wasn't too bad, considering.

It didn't take them long before they brought in a paper plate and, more importantly, a fresh hot mug of coffee with heavy cream and two strips of well-done bacon.

He was in heaven.

He righted himself, keeping the blanket covering his red, white, and blue boxers, the ones with the American flags and eagles printed all over it. With the paper plate on his knees, he began to dig in. It was scrumptious.

"You guys are too kind. This is awesome. I'm going to love you guys forever for this. You can cook for me anytime!"

Harper heard the pounding footsteps of Hamish coming down the stairs. He rattled all the windows in the house with his heavy gallop. His friend was over six foot four and nearly fifty pounds heavier than Harper. He had played rugby for many years, even going to college on a rugby scholarship. In the end, he blew out a knee and had to give up his school money. He signed on with the Navy on a conditional acceptance that he'd be medically discharged if the repair the Navy doctors did didn't bring him to at least eighty percent. They even allowed him to try out for the Teams after he'd done a few years and proved himself. He was one of the strongest members of SEAL Team 5.

"I can see the girls are taking good care of you. Sasha, honey, would you get me some coffee? I want to talk to Uncle Harper alone if you guys don't mind. Why don't you run along upstairs and get ready for the game. I think your mom is going to take you."

Hamish's coffee was brought to him, and the three girls disappeared upstairs.

Hamish took a big swig of his coffee and sat on an ottoman a few feet away from Harper. He checked his surroundings, satisfied that none of his family was nearby.

"So how did it go? I'm dying to know. Kyle told me you went to D.C.."

. "That ghost. I left him a message. I'm glad he got it. Yeah, I'm supposed to meet with him today, and I wanted to talk to you as well."

"I'm all ears. What's this about?"

"It's about an opportunity that came up, that was offered to me. And I don't know if you've ever thought about doing something else, but they're putting together a group of guys, and they want to operate it like a SEAL team. They want to have special operators from several groups to blend in all the skill sets. There are some Delta Force guys, group guys, paratroopers, rescue swimmers, two CIA operatives, and a few State Department special agents on the list. There are even a couple of women linguists and a female sniper from Team 8."

"Holy shit. What for?"

"They want older warriors with experience, guys who might be looking to retire, to give them support and create a specialized team they're calling Silver Team. They want to insert these people in small groups in areas not in the traditional way. It would be snatch and grab. They're after terrorists, disruptors who serve up mayhem, anarchists, and communists. The label isn't important. They want to catch these guys before they assemble their teams and get too powerful. Hit them when they're just getting started. They want to get the guys who turn some of our Universities into riot centers, threaten authority, destroy families, and try to tear down the fabric of society. The ones who train and teach bomb-making techniques to kids. Stuff like that."

"Scumbags, in other words."

Harper laughed. "That pretty much sums it up. They want to catch them before their money comes in. Sometimes, these kids come from wealthy families who never taught them values or gave them respect. They just like to hurt people, destroy neighborhoods. They are professional rabble-rousers in training, probably communist, Marxist, and they don't care about this country or anyone else's either. They maim and kill for fun. We've seen them, right?"

"Sure we have. So we'd be garbage collectors then."

"You could say that. But with one difference. We're to capture these guys, especially those who work with the young people, the university students, or the disenfranchised sons and daughters of public officials. Through kidnapping and blackmail, they try to strong-arm their way into society, bleeding out Marxist policies using terror and intimidation. They're looking for a team that will go in and extract these people and shut it down before it really gets a chance to start."

"And they asked you to be a part of this?"

"Hamish, I met with the president himself. Just like John Kennedy with the SEALs, this Silver Team is his baby."

"So you'd be working with the president?"

"No, hardly. It will have someone on the Joint Chiefs or one of the secretaries running it, probably Secretary of the Navy. They gave me a list of names, Hamish. Recommendations for people they thought might fit in."

Hamish took a huge gulp of his coffee and waited.

"Your name was number two on the list, Old Man."

Hamish stood up and walked to the window, over-looking his backyard and pool. Their youngest son was floating on a plastic donut, wearing goggles, diving for plastic rings and tossing them, then heading down to the bottom to retrieve them.

Harper could see it was an idyllic life, and he knew Hamish was thinking about how lucky these kids were and how he absolutely wanted to make sure that nothing ever got in the way of their happiness. He turned and caught Harper watching him.

"I got too much invested here, Harper. I mean, these guys are getting to the age where they're going to be leaving the house pretty soon. I only have so much time, and already being on Team 5, I'm gone nearly two hundred days a year. That's way more than we used to, remember?"

"Yeah, the world is blowing up big time. No question about that. But what if we had it set up so that we had support? So we didn't go to some of the more dangerous places? We actually have first-class weaponry and intel. We just need to do the infiltration quietly, but with the right to defend ourselves, of course. What if it wasn't like we were jumping into huge battles with the whole platoon? We are just going in to extricate the key players, maybe the top one or two, and then get out?"

Harper could see Hamish was seriously thinking about it. Part of him felt guilty for tempting him so.

"Of course, it's different for me. I don't have a family like you do, and that's something you have to think about. The price could be too high for you."

Just then, Hamish's wife came bounding down the stairs, followed by the girls.

"Oh, hi, Harper. I didn't know you were here."

"Babe, you were fast asleep when he texted me. It's just one night, okay? He's got a couple things to do here, and then he'll be going back home."

"Don't be silly. Harper is welcome here anytime. It's okay by us, isn't it, girls?" She turned, and all three of the girls giggled, Sasha putting her hands up to cover her braces while she did so.

Hamish stood, wrapped his huge tatted arms around his wife's pretty body, gave her a peck on the cheek, and waved goodbye. He also gave a kiss to Sasha.

As they began to file out of the front door, Hamish shouted, "By the way, girls, remember, you're not nice girls. You play tough, you play dirty, and if they give you any crap, you let them have it back double, you hear?"

Sasha laughed as the other two girls chimed in. "Yes, Sir."

"Love those girls," Hamish whispered, showing more emotion to Harper than he'd ever show the ladies in his life.

"My point, exactly, Hamish. Hell, you're practically man of the year down here. I'm embarrassed to even bring it up."

"Well, let me think about it. You meeting with Kyle today?"

"I am."

"So maybe I'll tagalong then. Would you mind that?"

"I don't mind at all. Can I ask you another favor?"

Hamish nodded his head. "Sure thing."

"Unless I can't see Kyle until late in the day, would you take me back to the airport afterwards so I can catch a four o'clock home?"

"You got it."

CHAPTER 9

HARPER PUSHED THE prospectus across the table and into Kyle's hands resting there.

"What's this?" his LPO asked.

"Look it over, Kyle. It's what they wanted to talk to me about."

Harper and Hamish sat across the table, side by side, facing Kyle. It was second breakfast for Harper. The Rusty Scupper was a favorite hangout of all the SEAL Teams in Coronado. Informal meetings would be conducted here, celebratory beers when someone got engaged or married or had a new baby. Even divorces were worthy of celebration, sometimes most joyful ones. All three SEALs had spent hundreds of hours with their brothers both inside and outside on the patio by the firepit.

As Kyle fingered the pages, Harper scanned the walls of the restaurant and bar. Covering every square inch available, both inside the bar, the main dining area, and the hallway leading to the back room where they sat were pictures of fallen brothers, as well as pictures of high-level targets they either captured or killed, campaign flags, and memorabilia from their various missions. A small Polaroid picture of a once head of state, infamous for capturing and torturing American warriors, as well as his own people, taken the day they found him in his underwear in a tunnel was still held up by a tack hammered all the way to the hilt.

Most of the photos or plaques had no explanation beneath them, because they weren't displayed for the general public. They were used to celebrate and leave a marker by various Team Guys who felt it was necessary to do so.

Over the bar was a long line of eight-by-ten glossy photos, usually taken on graduation day, SEALs in their brand-new white uniforms with their shiny new Tridents, wearing pillbox caps or officer attire. These were the ones who never made it home, and unlike the other pictures, their names were posted underneath. Everyone who sat at the bar got a good chance to study all the handsome young faces of guys who gave their all.

Just so no one would forget.

As Kyle continued to glance through the portfolio he read by section, thumbing through colorful tabs, Harper finished his eggs and raised his mug for another coffee, which was filled immediately. While reading, he whistled several times, pausing on certain paragraphs.

"Two hundred fifty per man, is that right?"

"Yup. It can go up from there, Kyle."

"No shit," mumbled Hamish.

"So they offered this team to you? I mean, is this already out there or are they creating it?" asked Kyle.

"I don't think they've done anything but this. They want me to help organize it if I'm interested. So, Kyle, am I interested?" Harper asked his LPO.

He glanced between Harper and Hamish then back to Harper. "You're going to drag Hamish into this too?"

"I promised you I'd talk to you first. I haven't made any promises to anybody. Scout's honor. I'm showing you and Hamish first. In the back, at the last tab, the little red one where it says Teams?"

Kyle flipped to the back and saw the list of names. He read his own name. "Kyle fucking Lansdowne. They got a lot of balls, Harper. They actually want you to recruit me, your LPO?"

"No, I don't want any part of being in command. I was going to offer you that position."

"I already have a Team, Harper. And you remember what I told you. I'm counting on you. I need you."

"Here's what I think, Kyle. There are some guys

who might be interested in this sort of thing, and I get it if you're not."

Kyle interrupted him. "I haven't even read the fucking thing. I mean, it's probably going to take me three days to do so. You're just springing this on me, and here I thought I was sending you off to go on a one and done; go find the asshole who killed Lydia."

Hamish punched Harper in the arm. "You fucking didn't tell me that, Sport."

"I did! Or I touched on it, Hamish. I'm going to tell you both everything I know now, but I'm on limited time. They want me to go overseas, accept the mission, go grab the guy, and bring him back so he can stand trial. The one we took down, Commander Okubo, he got what he deserved as he killed plenty of other people, but he's not the one responsible for Lydia's death."

Kyle's eyes sparkled. "So they get you with the prospect of going to even the score so to speak, they want you to lead this team knowing you have this burning desire to get rid of the asshole, and help them set up this new group in the process, is that right?"

"Yeah, that's about right. Apparently, they found him in Italy, And it's like you said, they figured it out. I killed the wrong guy, not that he didn't deserve it."

"Okay, so this is something I take it you have to do right away," Kyle asked.

"Yes, exactly. This guy apparently is assembling a terrorist cell, and the goal of this team, and they're going to call it Silver Team, the goal is to do a snatch and grab on him and bring him to a black site or the U.S.—and subject him to questioning try to find out where he's getting his equipment, his funds, all that sort of thing. We're supposed to bust up the whole gang. That's what they want. The salary they're offering is nearly double what we make on the Teams. I could certainly use the money. I don't have a family or anybody at home anymore, so I figured I might give it a shot."

"Oh, I understand it's tempting. That part got my attention."

"I want to stay on SEAL Team 3, and I'd probably re-up again if they'll let me do it, but you and I both know, Kyle, that jumping from airplanes and crawling around through snake-infested waters and fields or falling out of trees or getting hit by trucks or shot—I mean, there's only so much a human body can take. You know we've sent guys home in pieces or partially blinded or worse. You know we age faster than normal men. With the proper support, and the very best equipment, a well-organized small team each designed for a specific mission, which is what they say here, might not be a bad way to go. We watch out for each other, and of course, it's only as good as its weakest link, right?"

Harper could see Kyle was starting to pay more attention to his descriptions.

"So you didn't tell him you were going to quit Team 3 then, is that correct?" he asked.

"That's right, Kyle. I even got to talk to the President of the United States. It's his idea, like John Kennedy back in the 60s when he had the idea for creating the SEAL Teams."

"Thinks of himself as Kennedy, does he?" Kyle said cooly.

"How the hell should I know? But he wants to leave the recruitment up to me, although we would have a handler, and we would have liaisons and regular reports, perhaps meetings with him or perhaps with Admiral Patterson, who I also met with yesterday. He wants me to recruit and set it up. In this particular case, time's not on our side, so what I may do is take a small group over first then finish the setup back here in California."

"You want out of Team 3 that bad?" Kyle asked him.

"Absolutely not, Lanny. You're the best boss I've had. If it wasn't for you, I probably wouldn't be on a Team. This, though, seems to be something I might be able to do. I might be good at it. It's not a huge command. It's kind of loose, but with some training and ground rules, we could structure it so it was safe. We pick and choose who we wanted to use and veto anything they try to throw at us. We have to be super stealth about it. I did get permission to speak to both of you."

"Swell. How did they get my name?" Kyle asked.

"Reputation. Not only your name but Hamish's as well. We're all seniors here. That's why, but also we're solid guys with lots of experience. Both of you can be counted on to help keep me out of harm's way, basically. That's what the admiral said. There are other names on the list that I don't know so I'd have to sit and vet them carefully."

"You've got your work cut out for you." Hamish sighed.

"We'll have to see if there was enough interest to get a group to go over. If we take too long, he'll slip out of reach. It's taken them about a year and a half to find him. He doesn't stay in one place very long, has houses all over Italy, also in France, and even up in the Netherlands. Canary Islands too."

"So he was with the Okubo guys?"

"Apparently, he joined them for a few weeks in Africa, and he didn't like the situation with the militia group. So he went back to Italy where he's from and is working on setting his own team up. I was told they think he's planning terrorist attacks in Paris, Germany, and parts of Italy. Hitting tourist destinations or open-air markets, places where he could place bombs, terrorize certain communities. And part of the job is to infiltrate, get close to him, and then extract them and send them off when the time is right."

Kyle kept flipping through the pages, skimming some of the definitions, nodding here and there. Then, at last, he closed the book. Leaning over it, folding his hands, he looked directly into Harper's eyes, which made his blood freeze.

"I'm not interested. I would prefer that you not do this either, Harper. I think it's more dangerous than being on Team 3. But it's your decision, and I won't stand in your way if that's what you want. Only thing I ask is that you take a temporary leave, and they should be able to work that out for you. Then, if it doesn't work out, you come back to the Teams, unless you get injured or something. Does that sound fair?"

"Sure it's fair. But I'm also asking you, Kyle, should I do this? I mean, if you were in my shoes, would you?"

Kyle picked up his fork, slid it around the plate in front of him, then finally scooped up some scrambled eggs and popped them into his mouth. He chased them down with a few gulps of orange juice and then a sip of his coffee. The face he made told Harper the coffee was terrible without cream. Harper never trusted the coffee in these places, unless he had lots and lots of heavy cream to dilute it.

"In your situation, Harper, I think it's a good idea to try to get the guy. I think you'll sleep better. I think it's a good way to close that chapter. Maybe this is what you need in order to go on with your life. What do you think Lydia would want?"

Harper hadn't expected that question. He looked at Hamish, who was nodding his head, as if asking the same question.

Harper knew Lydia would not like it if he got himself in harm's way again, but she was still important to him, so prominent in his daily thoughts. He would have to say she haunted him, especially at night. So perhaps Kyle was right, and before he could get on with his life and perhaps find the next chapter among the living, he did need to get this resolved. The sniper was the monkey Harper needed to get off his back; he needed to make sure this guy was either dead and buried or captured and rotting in a cell somewhere.

"I think she'd say go for it. I honestly do. But I don't want to lose touch with you, Kyle—with both of you," he added, nodding to both his buddies.

"Of course. That's a given. I want you back, if you go, Harper. You'd probably have a hard time getting away from me," answered Kyle.

Harper was brightened from the inside out at that. He didn't want to impose. He didn't want to appear weak. But he also wanted to be successful, and Kyle could help a lot with that, in an unofficial capacity.

"You might find people who are getting ready to get out and might want to serve for a tour or two. Guys who've had a rough time. Maybe they'll allow us to rotate people through, that way we could get guys who are current in their skills, just wanting a change for a rotation or two. I'm not looking to decimate the Teams. I don't want to do that."

"It could work, Harper. Just one more option. You'd never get the Navy to create it on their own, but with some muscle from the president, and he was a Navy man, it gives warriors and those who support them another capacity to serve."

"I was told Kennedy got a lot of flak when he began planning for the SEAL Teams. Some branch jealousy, fighting over who would have jurisdiction. The Navy won out. I've been told that if Kennedy had been a group guy, it would have been Army all the way," Hamish added.

Kyle agreed. "Well then, I guess you have your answer. I can probably make some suggestions. Let me think about it, and I'll email you a list of guys I think might be good candidates, solid guys, some from other Teams and a couple guys that I know were flaming out on Team 3 who you haven't gone overseas with before. Men who want to serve but in a different capacity without the horror of taking on a desk job. There's nothing in the world worse than that for a man of action. Dead Man Walking."

"Amen to that, Brother," said Hamish.

Harper addressed his friend. "Same offer goes for you, although you're working up to deploy here in a couple of days. Think about it while you're gone, and when you get back, maybe I'll have it all set up. But you've already been recommended, so if you say yes, maybe we can get the same kind of deal worked out with your LPO, Hamish."

"Let me know if I can help, too, Hamish," added Kyle.

"I got to talk to Angie about it, though. I am not going to be able to commit until she's fully on board. But it sure does interest me, gets the juices flowing."

Harper put a hand on his shoulder and agreed. "I like the idea of getting good back up, the best equipment, and limited duty, days or weeks instead of months. And I also like the idea of not being stranded in the middle of the desert or in the jungles or plains in Africa. I've had enough of that. I like the low profile of it, so you think about it, Hamish."

"I will, Brother. I'll ask her, I'll let you know. I'll try to call you tomorrow, okay?"

"Fair enough."

"How's your dad?" asked Kyle.

"His dementia is progressing. That's also partly an issue here for me, because I may have to house him in a different facility, because he's getting into trouble. They've had to strap him in bed sometimes when he gets carried away. He's not sleeping regularly. Drawing on the walls. Every few minutes when I go there to visit him, he forgets who I am or where he is or what he was talking about. The only blessing in the whole thing is he really doesn't know he's going in and out of that. It's gone a little bit too far."

"That sucks, man," said Kyle.

"I don't really level with him, I just kind of play along. It's hard for me to see such a strong, dedicated, focused warrior melt into a frail, feeble-looking man who wears pajamas all day long and shuffles along the hallways in slippers."

Harper said his goodbyes to Kyle, promising he'd stay in touch and give him updates on what was happening with the team.

"I'm going to have to file some paperwork, so you let me know if you're for sure going to pull the trigger on this thing. Okay?"

"You bet."

Kyle looked up at Hamish, who towered over him, and delivered his parting shot. "I'm doing this because I want you to still stay on the Teams somehow. I don't know how they're going to work it out, but if you can come back, I want to keep that door open. I'm sure Grant over at Team 5 is not going to be happy when you talk to him. You might have to go in this upcoming deployment and then sit out the next one, so you give old Harper here a chance to show what kind of a miracle he can put off. But if you're getting any kind of pushback, because you're leaving so quickly, and you want to go now, I'm going to have to crack some heads."

"Understood, Sir."

"I'm doing this with a full heart and an open invitation to come back. And I don't care which team you come back to, I just don't want to be accused of diluting the teams for some kind of an experimental deal. We don't poach from each other's groups. We take people we need for short assignments. We do that all the time, especially on a temporary duty assignment. But we don't poach. So I'm only doing this, because I expect you'll come back, and you won't do it either."

"We're all on the same page, Kyle. If it's going to get fucked up, I'm out. I won't put you through that, Sir," said Hamish.

"Good. I want you to treat the Navy like the good friend it's been. It's not perfect, because it's made up of men and women who are imperfect by nature, but you owe them a lot for all the training and all the support they've given you over the years. You make sure you do this respectfully, and I don't want a shit storm. I especially don't want to create something that will jeopardize my retirement or advancement. You got it?"

Harper was getting slightly annoyed. "Hey, Kyle, how many times do we have to reassure you? Come on, Man."

"Until I'm convinced you're telling me the truth. Now get the Hell out of my sight," Kyle said as he pushed Harper in the chest.

They both jumped back into Hamish's truck, and they headed for the airport, leaving Kyle behind at the Rusty Scupper.

In the rearview mirror, Harper watched Kyle's body get smaller and smaller, until he could no longer make him out in the crush of tourists wandering up and down the strand.

The guy was a giant of a man. Harper would make sure he was protected, just as Kyle had done for him for over a decade.

CHAPTER 10

THE TWO FRIENDS embraced one last time at the departure gate.

"Hey, Man, don't sweat it. If your lady doesn't want any part of it, just figure it wasn't for you. No hard feelings either way."

"Honestly, Harper, I don't know what she'll say. I know she worries about me these days. Maybe she did when we were first together too, but she did a better job of covering it up. Funny how old age changes things, doesn't it?"

That particular comment hit Harper like a frozen wave. He had no one in his life, not anymore, and he'd only had her for a few years. He didn't know what it was like to be a father or husband long term. But Hamish didn't mean anything by it, so Harper just grinned and let it slide.

"Well, you're a lucky man, Hamish. Those kids of yours, they're genuine works of art. They need you.

Don't do anything to jeopardize that."

"Tell me honestly, Harper. You think it will be less dangerous?"

"You know the answer to that, Hamish. You could get hit by a bus on the way home today. Nothing's for certain, right? I think Kyle's right about the fact that there's that unfinished part of my life that I have to tackle. I'm going to surround myself with a few people I'm going to feel good about going into battle with. Otherwise, they don't make the team. If it gets something too complicated, or I don't have enough control, then it's not for me, and I'll come back to Team 3. Kyle said he'd take me back. That's the only lifeline I need at this point."

"Yeah, as long as the Navy does. You know what you're doing. I kind of envy the fact that you don't have roots."

"Now, don't you dare envy that, Hamish. I've got Venom and my neighbor, Sally, and all you guys. That's it. No family, no wife, girlfriends, kids. One small exception is one of Sally's friends teaches yoga at the beach at sunset. But I'm not ready. In a way, that's how I realized I needed to excise some demons first. Shit, Hamish, I'm too scared to engage."

Hamish chucked.

"I just think there's something for me out there. I owe it to Lydia to grab that guy, and then maybe, just then, I can let it all go."

Hamish grabbed him and squeezed his torso so hard it nearly busted a rib or two. "You take care of yourself, Brother. You're a national treasure. Don't forget it. Make it count."

Harper didn't turn around as he swung the duffel bag and computer case over his shoulder. Truth was, his eyes were watering. He was so fucking lonely, nothing a couple of good nights' sleep, some heavy gardening, doing repairs in the yard, and painting could fix. Not tonight, but tomorrow or the next day, maybe he'd go out to the ocean and see if Evie was there. But only if it was right. And now, just going home was the rightest thing he could do.

While he waited to board, he called Sally.

"Oh, glad you're coming today. Does this mean I don't have to stay up until midnight or two a.m.?"

"That's what it means. Venom give you any trouble?"

"Oh my God, no! Perfect gentleman. Eats like a horse, he stays right by my side, even following me into the bathroom. He and I are a team. We both know I'm second best, but it's the best we can do for right now. I know he'd rather be with you."

"Isn't that the way of the world, Sally? Nobody gets one hundred percent of what they want."

"But you always get what you need."

Harper laughed at the reference to the Stones' song. He'd always liked that song.

Next call he made was to Admiral Patterson. "Sir, I've talked to my LPO. Kyle thinks he can spare me, but he doesn't want to let me go. I'm trying to work out something, so that if this doesn't work out with the Silver Team, I can come back. Is there any reason that wouldn't work?"

"I don't see why not. But we certainly don't want to set something up, put money and assets into it, and then have you turn around and bail on us. I don't think you'd do that."

"To be honest, I owe him a great deal. He's saved my life a couple of times at least, and I don't think there's any harm by saying that if I discover it's not for me I'd rather not have to start flipping burgers or making coffee at Starbucks. This would give us all the best possible solution."

"But you're leaning into making it work."

"I am."

"Give me your number one reason you'd want to go back."

"Expectations too heavy. Not enough under my control. Personalities of the team and me clashing. Not being able to boot someone I don't want there. There's always something that makes you second guess, Sir."

"That's for sure. But the money is good. That

help?"

"With my dad, temporarily, yes. But I owe it to Lydia to catch the asshole who took her away from me. My biggest problem is not catching the guy. It's going to be hard as hell if I have to bring him back alive."

"Roger that, Harper. You, you're working on it? Can I tell the president this?"

"Give it until tomorrow morning. I'll be sure to give you a call first thing."

"Thanks, Son. You have a good evening, and safe travels."

IT WAS ONE of the easiest flights home he'd had in a long time. He'd been bumped up to first class, and even in the small plane, two whiskeys later, he was feeling fine and knew he'd have to stop somewhere in the airport for some food before driving home.

Venom was beside himself with excitement, attempting to lick Harper's nose or give him a slobbery kiss across his chops. Harper was still hungry, so he barbequed two steaks, one for him and one for Venom. Venom's was gone before Harper could lay his napkin on his lap and begin cutting the meat.

He walked around the house and then out into the upper part of the garden and made his list of things he wanted to do tomorrow. He picked some flowers to put on the marble bathroom counter, right next to Lydia's toothbrush, pretending he'd get to watch her enjoy them.

Sally had converted some photographs and videos to a recorded DVD and gave it to him after Lydia's funeral. She'd retrieved the images from her phone, which came in the box from the mission, along with her washed and folded clothes and a spiral notebook. Sally had asked permission first, and Harper hadn't minded.

He'd never watched it before.

Slipping the disc into the player, he showered, donned his pajamas, then sat back in the bed, Venom stretched out alongside him, and turned on the player.

Lydia's name came up on the screen, surrounded by flowers. Sally had chosen some light guitar music for background, and one by one, he watched the images of them walking the beach with Venom, Venom chasing sticks Harper threw into the surf, along with some cute videos of the back of his ass as she followed behind him at the Farmers' Market.

The sweeping view of the market and the colorful fruit and vegetable vendors also showed a brief clip of his face, full of love, and looking much happier and even younger.

The ache in his heart started to pulse. Taking deep breaths forced the tears in his eyes to stop spilling over his lower lids.

They'd attended a SEAL wedding down at the beach in Coronado. Under golden glow from hundreds of candles stuck in the sand, they danced and laughed so much his sides ached. Their own wedding had been simple, quick, and done at the courthouse because his deployment was coming up the next day. He'd told her he'd be damned if he'd go off to the jungle and not have her properly married with a ring on her finger, his ring. He'd told her she would never be able to leave him. She had said the same too.

The last few pictures were of the mission in Benin. She loved taking shots of the children with their big eyes and wide smiles. She played with a stethoscope with several of the children, sharing the chance to hear each other's heartbeat.

The mission crew was sort of rag-tag. She'd told him by phone that several of the staff came from Belgium, spoke French, and were part of a large evangelical Christian organization that was popular there, taking after the missionary work of Dr. Schweitzer. One by one, she photographed the five doctors and twelve aides and nurses who had accompanied them.

There was also a mission teacher, a young man who nearly always had his back turned to the camera. She'd snuck around the front of him and surprised him with a full shot of his face. He was a handsome fellow, and it bothered him that this man, as well as the others, were the last to see her alive. His dark brown curly hair was long enough to pull back in a ponytail. His eyes were wide and dark brown.

Harper wondered about the survivors and who must have taken the pictures of the aftermath. He was going to see if he could find out. That brought up other questions, like, how many did survive? Were they aid workers or natives? How did they survive?

The last part of the reel was a nice photo of her grave Sally must have taken herself with Lydia's phone. Venom sat next to him, studying the flowers resident there.

It was getting easier to look at photos of Lydia, except for the one.

One day at a time, he thought. But he doubted there would ever be a day when he didn't feel that ache in his chest, as if her passing had forever physically altered his body.

And he'd never be the same.

CHAPTER 11

HARPER GOT UP at the crack of dawn, going for a run with Venom at his side. He managed to take on the hills first, then move to the lower areas of his property, down below Sally's plot. He'd created criss-crossed running trails, protected with crushed granite, making a pleasant swoosh, swoosh sound as his feet lightly danced on the path ahead.

He paced himself, attempting to not draw any attention to his sprinting. The woods were just beginning to come alive. A few birds were already out, foraging for food or flying above in search of breakfast.

From his driveway, there was a palpable sound of the town he overlooked, Santa Rosa, almost like it was a steam engine that had started to rev up. It was a blank space type of sound. From years living there, he knew that, as the day wore on, the sound would grow louder and incorporate equipment noises, traffic, and horns. But right now, he heard that hush as he looked toward the horizon. That's the best way he could describe it. Hush, like mother nature was holding her breath, waiting for somebody to pierce the air with a scream or a cat call of some kind.

He regulated his breathing, doing the box breathing exercises he'd been trained. He kept the same rhythm even as he ran up or downhill. By pushing himself in this way, he got the maximum workout possible.

Once back at the house, he heard sounds of Sally mucking around in her kitchen and soon smelled scents unique to her breakfast. She liked to cook bacon or other fresh meats, and it smelled so good he was about ready to crash in her door and give himself an invite.

But he had a lot to do today. After viewing the video last night, he'd sat propped up in his bed staring at the blank screen. Just thinking. Now that he was involved in the mission to get hold of Lydia's killer, he was more plugged in. He noticed little details in those pictures, especially the ones at the end, and he used those to spur on his healthy curiosity in order to figure out what he did not know. It felt like he'd been there during the slaughter.

Harper learned long ago that it was crucial a group of men working together find out what they did not know so they wouldn't be blindsided. It was okay to guess or make a decision based on valid information. But to not be curious, to not research and come to an accurate conclusion could cause great harm, not only to himself but all the others on the team. And anything that was assumed about the players, the intel, or the Team without verification was just plain foolish and could cost lives. He was to be prepared for everything, even the stuff that was unexpected. The objective was to achieve the mission no matter what.

He reviewed the list of suggestions Admiral Patterson had given him while he was waiting for his eggs to cook. Most of the names had email addresses and phone numbers, which made it easier for him. He knew the first two on the list, Kyle and Hamish, would be talking to him at some point in the morning. The rest of the men were not close personal friends. Some of them, he had met but not on a mission.

There simply wasn't time to fly to Virginia Beach or down to Coronado to individually interview these men, though, and that bothered him. It was taking a risk. Harper was going to have to do it over the phone, approve and make the difficult choices, perhaps approve a larger group, and then cut back from there.

Harper left a message for one individual. As he was hanging up, Hamish was calling in on the other line.

"Well, I'm not sure if I'm going to be divorced or if we're going to continue on for another twenty years or so, Harper, but she cried. It was 'no' last night, but this morning, she said she wanted me to go, but only on the condition that you were going too, Harper."

"That's good news. Should we wait another day to see if she changes her mind or are you set?"

"No, I'm set. We don't go back and forth that way."

"So what about your LPO?"

"I've already called for a meeting. I suppose it's okay to tell him what we're trying to do? I mean he is Navy, and I'm going to encourage him to talk to Kyle."

"That's a good idea. You're going to see him today then?"

"Have to. We're leaving like day after tomorrow. I'm out of time."

"Good deal. Well, you get to working on that. I want you to make a list of your must-haves as far as firepower and any specialized equipment or explosives you would like to work with. I wanted it all laid out ahead of time for the entire team so they can get our provisions in one delivery."

"Where are we going to be stationed? Do you know that yet? Are we going to have our own team building like they do here?"

"No clue. What I've got is not much. I'll be getting more later tomorrow, I presume. I'm to be calling Patterson every day. If we had to, there're places up here we could use. But I think it makes more sense to be close to where everybody lives, and that's probably going to be Coronado. I'll ask for permission to use the Team 3 building since so many of us have passes for it."

"Makes perfect sense. I'm going to help my better half and then get myself presentable for my meeting. Fingers crossed here."

"You'll need more than luck, Hamish. How are your nerves?"

"To tell you the truth, Harper, I had a hard time last night. I couldn't sleep a wink. Not nerves really, I'm jazzed about this whole thing. I'm as excited as I was on my first deployment. I was such a dumb son of a bitch. Maybe I'm doing that again."

By the time Harper had called several names he knew to be on West Coast teams, he had filled his limit, thinking the first trip out he would only take a team of eight. He would take two shooters, and he was going to be one of those; two medics; possibly a linguist, depending on where they were going; a coms person; and two explosive Ordinance Handlers. He checked and cross-checked to make sure every man he called had a specialty or two, preferably more than two. If one of them got injured or was out of commission during an op, someone else could step into their shoes and complete the work that needed to be done. Cross training, having the right combination of trained team members, was a must and was the secret of success for their former Team 3.

Harper gave Admiral Patterson a call to let him know they were in, and the admiral agreed to send over several contracts: one for him, one for Hamish, and several blank contracts for the others to review. The salaries, certain terms of employment, and confidentiality clauses were all spelled out in detail. He just had to fill in the names.

"What about Kyle?" Patterson asked.

"No deal. Kyle's not ready to give up his position. I think he wants to let us make all the mistakes first before he jumps in. But eventually, it would be good to have him. We'll work on it for the future."

"I'm sorry to hear that, Harper. We were kind of hoping he'd say yes."

"It's not a definite no. It's just a no for now. I've been making my calls, and I think I have a good group we can use. Kyle's going to keep his eyes open for new candidates that we might be able to recruit later, if we need it, people who have been tested and whom he trusts."

"That's smart on his part. He wants to make sure that you guys leave on good terms so he can get you back if it doesn't work. That's a valid plan."

Patterson indicated he was also going to send overnight new photographs of the location of Mr. Lipori and several of his new recruits.

"Good, because that one photo was rather grainy, hard to tell what anyone looked like."

"Also, you'll be flying into Florence, to a little area to the south west."

"Italy? That surprises me."

"Lipori is an Italian name, Harper. He's an Italian national. It's nice vineyard and olive tree farming area. Gentle rolling hills, very old villas, many of them in horrible disrepair. We're going to rent you guys an apartment in town and a house out in the country, which happens to be very close to the Lipori Villa. In this way, you're going to be able to track his movements. The apartment is on the main drag, right at the entrance to the village square, so you will be uniquely able to follow him from his house right into downtown where he would be shopping. There's also a vegetable market every Friday that he usually goes to when he's home. They sell fresh vegetables from the farm, olives, when in season, and olive oil. He has staff at the villa as well: a couple of cooks, a handyman, couple of housekeeping staff, and several groundskeepers. There's a lot of activity going on during the day, not too much at night. He seems to keep to himself, at least that's what our intel says."

"What kind of an asset do you have in place doing all this reconnaissance?"

"He's a retired Italian Special Forces dude. A patriot. He has a delivery service, bringing supplies to several of the elderly residents who live outside the city limits."

"How'd you get him?"

"He's a friend. One of the Teams rescued his granddaughter in North Africa during a terrorist takeover of the Italian embassy. He's a grateful man and a good friend to Uncle Sam."

"Good deal. I can certainly trust a guy like that. And by the way, I'm sending you a list of required items, once I get the info from everyone, like you asked. I'm assuming everybody brings their own sidearm and whatever long gun they're used to, or do you want to issue those to us?"

"No, I want you to use your own firearms. We'll supply all the ammunition, of course, but everybody comes armed, your weapons maintained and freshly cleaned. If you've got anything that is not working properly, let me know, and we'll get you a replacement to switch it out."

They discussed their timeline, and it was agreed seven days from today would be the day they'd gather at Coronado and take a transport plane to the East Coast, at Norfolk, and then make the huge leap to Italy. From there, they would rent several cars and a van to transport all the equipment.

By early afternoon, he still hadn't heard from Kyle. He called one more time and left his third message of the day. Hamish called to give him an update from his meeting and indicated Kyle had helped with the paperwork. He was cleared to go and would be picking up the signatures in the morning.

"Kyle says he'll send you the paperwork from his office, so when you come down here, he'll finalize it and we can turn everything in."

Satisfied that they'd done everything they could, he began to work on the little repair items and the gardening. He cleared a patch for growing a new crop of lettuce and cold crops, trimmed off several blossoms on his pear, Asian pear, and apple trees. He decided next he needed to talk to Sally about taking care of Venom while he'd be away.

He ran down the driveway until he came to her house, slightly over a mile. Venom sat next to him while he knocked on Sally's door.

She must've been painting because she wore a smock that was blotched with brightly colored streaks. She had her hair up with a bandanna, holding it off her forehead.

"You should've told me you were coming. I would've taken off all these paint clothes, fixed us something. What's up?"

"I'm going to be taking a group overseas. We're

going to leave in about seven days, Sally, and I was wondering if you'd be willing to watch Venom again."

"Boy, they work you pretty hard, Son. How long will you be gone?"

"I'm guessing two weeks but subject to change. We're not sure. Our target will be there, so it could get delayed if we can't find him."

"So you're saying next Saturday sometime?"

"Yes. I'll bring him down with his food and couple of toys on Friday. Also bring his dog bed."

"No problem, Harper. You be careful, though. Are you going with the whole team?"

Harper was careful not to divulge more than he should so he indicated to her that yes, he was going with the rest of the team. He wasn't going to tell her it was a different team than he had served with the last nearly ten years. But he explained also that it was a short, temporary assignment and that the idea was to get in and get out quickly.

"Well, Venom and I will hang out here. He's going to miss you again. I don't think you've ever been gone so soon after you came back. But he'll survive."

Harper knelt down, scratched Venom's ears, then stroked his head from his neck down to his butt.

"You're such a good boy, Venom. You like staying with Aunt Sally, don't you?"

His intelligent soul stared at him stoically, then

searched Sally, and then turned back to study Harper again. He knew something was up. Harper stroked him again and let him know that yes, he was going to miss him as well.

Early in the morning, a little bit after one, Harper got a call from Admiral Patterson.

"We've located him. It's a positive ID. I've secured the rentals for you, and we're arranging the vehicles."

"Why the early morning call? You could have called me tomorrow at a later time," Harper asked.

"Because we believe they're going to be taking a trip and wanted to make sure you were ready, just in case we have to leave early. They move around a lot, and he's just had a whole group of military-age males arrive at the villa. We have our guy on it, and I'll get some pictures for you and send them over. If I get them before I send out the contracts, I'll make sure to include them."

"Any idea what kind of activity they're going to do?" Harper asked.

"It's definitely a bomb. They've been picking up fertilizers and some metal containers, all stuff they'd use for a huge bomb, something showy. Near a large population area. Only thing that will be well-populated will be the market on Friday. There aren't any festivals planned. But the market will blow their cover. We assume it will be somewhere else."

"Wouldn't they head to a larger city?"

"We don't believe they're going to travel very far with all that liquid they have to transport. Stuff's not stable, either. But we understand they do have plans to leave. I think we are going to cut off contact just to make sure he doesn't wind up checking over his shoulder and get spooked. We want you to have the optimum result."

"Thank you, Sir."

"One other thing. I did get a couple calls from three of your guys, and I had to reassure them that the money was real and that I would be depositing funds in everyone's account tomorrow. I just wanted you to know, Harper. Are you sure about everyone you've chosen?"

"Can't give you a hundred percent, Admiral. Most of them have never met me before. Until that happens, we're a little stuck."

"If you're not solid about any of them, I want you to pull them before you go."

"Will do. So if there isn't anything else, can I get back to sleep?"

CHAPTER 12

HARPER WAITED IN the hanger in Coronado for the rest of his team to show up. Earlier in the day before he hopped on the flight from Santa Rosa, he'd said one final goodbye to his father and rewarded Venom with another steak dinner last night. He took the time to care for what was left of his family: His dad and Venom. He combed and petted the dog, speaking to him in hushed tones before he took him down to spend the night at Sally's, since he was to leave early in the morning.

His dad that evening was the same as he'd been the time before, but without the restraints. He even managed to get an appointment with his father's doctor.

"I know you're concerned about what the next step is here, options being limited. I really think he's still able to be reasoned with, Harper. Rather than placing him in one of our quiet rooms, a holding cell for lack of a better word, I think we should explore other options.

I think a cell would be tremendously demeaning to him, and he might mistake the experience as going to jail. I'm going to recommend, instead, that we up his meds and perhaps take away his desire to be so active."

"Doesn't seem fair."

"But it's the safest for him. You don't want to let him spend his days throwing feces, do you? If he gets into that routine, you'll never be able to trust taking him places in public. It would be the end of his social life, Harper. There are lots of new drugs that just take away that need to break out and act up, without turning him into a Zombie. I'd like to try a few, if you don't mind."

"If you honestly think it will keep him safer and out of confusing mental pain, Doctor."

"I do, Harper. At this point, his dementia has progressed so far that it's like a rubber band that's been overstretched. It's not going to go back. I wouldn't hold out any hope that he will improve. If we see a clinical trial coming down the line I think we should try, I will make sure to put his name in for a testing trial."

Harper had been satisfied with his report, explained to the doctor that he would be out of the country, and gave them Sally's phone number in case some emergency befell his dad.

"You can also try calling me, as I believe I will have

cell service. But I may not be able to talk, and I certainly can't come home to handle anything."

Now, as he sat in the hangar, all the planning and preparation and the interviews he conducted with the team gave him a renewed sense of hope. He was satisfied that he'd done all he could do, for now. He believed he got all the right players, and he was anxious to get the mission started.

He even surprised himself. He was the "no leadership" guy, the one who never wanted to be in charge, who preferred to make things happen for another leader. But this prospect, this team, gave him some of his old excitement he used to feel on Team 3 and others he'd served on.

He mentally reviewed his team qualifications.

He'd recruited Sean Daly, the old man of the group at nearly fifty years of age, an explosives expert from SEAL Team 5. Paul Taylor from his own Team 3 was his second, with a special interest in making odd-looking devices the enemy thought were lethal when they weren't. He and Calvin "Coop" Cooper from Team 3 had made a challenge of it, trying to better each other, much to the Team's delight. Harper was glad Paul had decided to come along, although he told Kyle, if it wasn't "perfect," he was coming back to Team 3. Harper would take him anyhow, because he was easy to work with and damned smart.

Sam Hobbs from SEAL Team 3 was his coms guy, but he could second as a sniper. He also was good with throwing hatchets and knives and created his own designs that were wicked-looking, only selling them to Team Guys. Knute Thayer was one medic, and Caesar Goya was the second. Both these men were recruited/recommended from SEAL Team 3. Both were ten-year men and had experienced lots of bloody combat. Kyle had mentioned they were on their way out and looking for a command they could still participate in. They were best friends and had daughters in college they were struggling to pay for. The extra money was a godsend.

Carl Womack was the other sniper from SEAL Team 3 and rounded out the group with Hamish McDougall, also an explosives expert. Carl had come through a nasty divorce and had been considering transferring to Team 4 on the East Coast, until Kyle talked him into working with Silver Team. He had never wanted to leave Coronado anyway. Harper had already joked with him that he'd made a good decision, since, in Harper's opinion, it was easier to pick up girls in California than Little Creek.

He was looking forward to working with these men, and the fact that they had been prior vetted and made the list, probably by somebody from a West Coast Team, made Harper feel more comfortable.

They were starting already to feel like family. That was important.

Other players might be picked up for the Silver Team project later on. He knew there were a couple of great CIA assets as well as State Department special agents, and there could be a time when these would be important to a team. But for right now, just to keep things simple, he wanted everyone to have been in the same kind of training, the same level of knowledge, and already used to working together as a team over and over and over again, which was the strongest thing about their SEAL community.

Carl Womack arrived with Caesar Goya, introducing themselves and setting their duffel bags down on the floor. Carl brought a large special case for his long gun.

"Welcome, Gentlemen. We're going to have some fun, aren't we?"

Caesar had questions. "So it's Italy? They say it's Italy, right?"

"Yes. I will have a briefing on the plane, if we can hear. The guy we're looking for is Jakob Lipori, who also has solid terrorist bona fides. A dangerous dude for sure."

"So is this a capture or kill?" asked Womack.

"It's capture. They want to try them in U.S. Military court for atrocities. I'm not sure if I told all of you, but Mr. Lipori is the sniper responsible for the death of my wife. Some of you, I told this to on the phone, while others I didn't, so there it is. And I'm okay if you tell others. Once we get to Italy, though, we're going to be on complete silence. Nothing that we do here in the States is going to be spoken about overseas. We always did that when we went to the Middle East and Africa. I see no reason to change that rule just because we're in a NATO country. It's just as dangerous, and it could be just as crucial for the success of the team."

"Oh, I hear you, Boss. I'm in total agreement with that," said Carl.

Paul Taylor and Hamish arrived next. It was a natural occurrence that all of the men who had been trained on SEAL Teams would semicircle, rearranging the chairs. It was their way of sharing information and discussing things without leaving anybody out. Knute and Caesar compared medic bags and medic packs, discussing a couple of things they might want to pick up when they got to Norfolk. Harper said he'd make sure they had what they needed by the time they landed and sent a text to Patterson to make sure it was going to happen.

Sam Hobbs and Sean Daly were friends, married to twin sisters. Hobbs was on SEAL Team 3, and Daly was on SEAL Team 5. They had told Harper they were looking forward to finally getting to work together after both of them being on the teams over fifteen years. Their experience almost eclipsed that of Harper's.

They loaded up and quickly took off for Norfolk. The interior of the transport was so rattling and noisy it made the discussion Harper was going to have impossible. The next leg of the trip was in a commercial jet, and they had the entire plane to themselves. These were the jets used to transport migrants from the border to various cities throughout the United States and, in some cases, deport them.

He went over the plan, the assignments as far as who was going to stay where. Harper put three people in the house in Imprunetta, the little village they were staying at outside of Florence, and he put five, including himself, at the villa.

He showed the men all the areas where Lipori had been seen and showed on a map of the town where the market was on Fridays, which would be a good way to informally get information and perhaps speak with the man or parts of his staff. Any extra intel or information they could dig up would help later when they made the extraction.

"I've been told we can bring him back by any means necessary, including medical inducement. We are not to cause death. And we want to especially be careful about any of the innocents that he may have in his employment. If there is any resistance, then those individuals will have to be arrested, and we'll let the Navy sort it out later. We have absolute authority to be able to bring anybody of interest to the United States. This has all been approved in advance by our State Department. You don't have to concern yourself about international law, as far as we know. That said, things happen, but that's the plan," he finished.

There were a few questions, the smattering of jokes, and some casual banter, but Harper liked the way the Team held together. It seemed to have a cohesive jelling quality to it, everyone was cooperative, and he didn't pick out any red flags or social media misbehavior. He also recommended no one go off and do anything by themselves, which would leave himself and the rest of the team very vulnerable.

"You want to go in pairs everywhere, ideally threes or fours. I think you could pose as tourists, because we are only going to be there for a short period of time. It's okay to be identified as American."

"Any suggestions on the pronouns we should use?" asked Sean. Everyone chuckled.

"In your case, Sean, it's 'It, Me, and Fuck Off.' Got it?"

"I'm crystal clear with that, Boss. Just keeping us straight."

"And we protect all colors, creeds, and shoe sizes.

The gender thing I'm having a problem with right now, but I'll tell you if I'm able to figure it out."

It was always good when the Team Leader had the group laugh at his jokes. Harper watched as the guys gave him that, and more.

"You can flirt with girls. You just don't want to flirt with any of the authorities, especially the Italian police."

They landed in Florence just as the sun was setting. It was a gorgeous approach to the city proper with a pinkish purple sky as a background to the red brick and tile roofed buildings and golden church spires. Florence was a big city with a dynamic but dangerous city center.

After they loaded up in their rental vehicles, which surprisingly took little time, they headed west into the rural farming areas and small villages encircling the Florence area. There were very few huge farms or conglomerates, the largest being wineries with vines extending forever in neat rows trailing up over the gentle sloping hills. It reminded Harper of scenes from Sonoma County where he grew up.

Unlike most U.S. cities, Florence was steeped in over a thousand years of history. The powerful Medici family had made an imprint on the whole region that remained to this day. They had contributed museums, cathedrals, libraries, and large state buildings. All kinds of unique architecture filled the city, full of culture and some of the finest collections of paintings in the world. But once their travels took them outside into the rural area, that's where Harper's chest began to relax, and he was able to breathe the fresh country air. Life wasn't hurried here. Frequently they had to slowly travel behind a tractor or a wooden cart pulled by a donkey that had no room to pull over or go around.

They found people of all ages, including the elderly, used bicycles close to town. The young kids used electric bikes and sometimes skateboards or small scooters. Along the road, they passed clusters of students on scooters, sometimes all girls and sometimes mixed couples. In the little town of Imprunetta, there were several delis downtown they hit up first, since both the house and the apartment came unstocked with anything other than just basic necessities.

In two separate groups, they went shopping. Some looked for meat and deli items, cheeses, special sausages, bologna, and fruits in season. The other group went on a quest for bakery items, sweets, and bread for sandwiches. Hamish picked up the milk products that they would need, primarily half-and-half for their coffee and fresh ground Italian roast coffee for the coffee maker that was supposed to be provided in both locations. He also picked up condiments for their barbecues, since at the little house, it was touted as having a huge fire pit and barbecue area.

They ate in the apartment in Imprunetta, and then the five of them came to the house and set up house-keeping there. Harper told them they should double check all their equipment, get their chargers up and running, and make sure the batteries were full before turning in. The next day was to be a day of exploring around the small village and surrounding areas, investigating, and getting a feel for the region and some of the businesses and people who lived and worked there. Harper was to meet with Leonardo, the former Italian Special Forces friend of Uncle Sam.

He retrieved his night vision goggles and watched the villa. He spotted Lipori right away, moving around and giving orders. Then later, he heard music and saw several men drinking wine and eating pizza on folding tables in the driveway just outside the rear door to the building. They had created a huge fire in an oversized fire pit, large enough to grill a wild boar.

He switched scopes so the light from the fire didn't bleed in and ruin the picture. He tried to photograph the crowd and was pleased that some of the faces came through, so he sent them upstairs to Patterson. He scanned all of them one by one but did not see Lipori.

Patterson texted him the same comment.

Harper let him know he'd seen Lipori earlier, but he kept looking.

One of the things he noticed was that all of the military-age males appeared to come from different countries. They didn't appear to be Italian, even though he knew some northern Italians were blonde and blue-eyed. Some looked Scandinavian while some appeared Ukranian or from the Baltic regions. And there were two Africans, with everybody else in between.

On a final sweep of the area, he again saw the silhouette of Lipori, and judging from his gait, he appeared to be irritated and in a hurry. It was funny, Harper thought, how they've been trained to pick out the leader of a group, and this guy definitely was the group leader, the other team members showing him deference.

Eventually, one by one, all of the men went inside. There were no women present. Harper figured the staff went to their own homes at night, especially with the influx of so many of these new males.

Beyond the villa was a what looked like an old stable that had a roof line that had collapsed. Debris, rubble from the cobblestones had fallen apart. And next to the stable was a beautiful vegetable garden appearing to be more than a half-acre. Rows were very evenly kept. Not a single weed in the place. Harper was in awe of the beautiful garden, parts of it glowing in the partial moonlight from above. It was hard to see, but he thought he saw a huge flower garden in the rear.

He walked outside to look at the stars and could hear faint sirens running in all directions. He also heard discussions in Italian floating and carrying over the hills, bouncing down the bottom of the canyon and up the other side. He made a note to himself to mention that to the men. The acoustics were such that the whole area turned into a large acoustical bowl. If they weren't careful, they could be heard two or three miles away.

Harper was ready for bed. He opened the envelope that contained contracts and extra photographs Patterson had sent just before he left the house in California. He flipped through them one by one, examining the face of this young terrorist who was out for so much death and destruction. He wondered what made a person like that. He was a handsome man, with long brown hair that could be pulled back into a ponytail. He was tanned and smiled a lot with big white teeth. If he didn't know better, he'd think he was a college kid somewhere local, kicking around the little village on spring break.

And then something caught his eye about Lipori's picture. He noted the man had a necklace, a tribal necklace. On the surface was carved a face tied to a leather strap worn around his neck. Somewhere he had seen that necklace before. Perhaps he'd seen it in one of the shops at the airport or in the village, but he thought not. It did look African. Perhaps this was from his African days with the warlord's Merry Band of Bandits.

It continued to bug him. All of a sudden, the side view of Lipori came up, and he saw what appeared to be something hidden beneath his shirt and knew that he had seen this before somewhere. His face appeared to resemble the man who lifted Lydia's lifeless body up to transport her in the back of a truck. Searching back-and-forth from his computer screen to the photos, he became more and more certain of it.

Now he realized where else he'd seen this man before. He was the aid worker who appeared at the end of Sally's Lydia tribute. He didn't bring the CD with him, just the shot of Lydia being lifted. That had been Lipori. Was he one of the aid staff? Maybe there was more to the story than they'd told him. Could it be that Lydia actually knew her killer? Did something occur that turned him, suddenly, into a terrorist?

He laid back on the pillow, closed his eyes, and saw some of the happy images of Lydia and him walking with Venom on the beach.

"I'll always love you, Lydia. I'll never give up until I get this guy. Nothing else in my life is as important as that. I promise."

CHAPTER 13

NEXT MORNING, HARPER got the text back from Patterson with a response to the information he'd sent to him in D.C.. He called Patterson's cell.

"What are you thinking?" Patterson asked.

"She knew him. I have a video of them talking. She took that video the day she was killed."

"I need to get that."

"Working on it. Does this mean we just go in there and pick him up?"

"We know they plan to leave. He's bought a ticket to London. I don't have the other names. That's not until next week. Do you have anything on him we can arrest him for?"

"Hardly," Harper scoffed. "We just got here yesterday. We need a little more time. But doesn't this change things? We can prove he knew my wife now. That he'd been planning something. Won't that be enough?"

"Then you have to find something. Even if it's an expired passport, something we can hold him on. Evidence of bomb-making material would be perfect."

"Why not try for a miracle as well? We'll have to dig around. I was just hoping this was enough."

"I have to see the proof. Even then, probably not."

"I'll get my friend to forward the CD she made. You'll see it at the end."

"Okay, good. You'll need to get pictures inside the house, check out their cars, see if you can find some form of ID so we can run traces on who the others are."

"Like you saw from the pictures, they're a mixed bag, young kids from all over the world."

"Not uncommon for first-class recruiters. Any flags, t-shirts with writing, posters, or anything?"

"Not without rummaging through their drawers. We'll get inside tomorrow."

"Excellent."

"I wish I knew how many people were in the villa. I mean, we just got here yesterday, and it's not enough time as far as gathering information. The element of surprise would be on our side, but I just don't want to get blindsided by going in there and finding out there were more people than we thought. Now on the other hand, if another load of males happen to show up at the villa, then we'd be screwed."

"Well, in that case, we probably have to initiate something else. Although I think any of you could handle probably a couple dozen, I just don't think it's a good idea until you have all the information. I'll roll with whatever you think. It's probably not a good idea to contact the president yet, but I'll leave that up to you. We don't have anything definitive, other than the theory he slipped in under an alias."

"I concur. I think we ought to wait and know exactly who's there. See if you can identify any of those pictures I sent. If you need something more specific, like you need one particular guy's close-up or something, you let me know and we'll try to get her done. I have a high-powered lens that does remarkably well, so if you need something in more detail, just let me know."

"Will do. I'll get working on those photos right away. With the face recognition software, it should be a piece of cake."

"One additional thing, Admiral. The guy, Lipori, the shooter—is there any chance that we're wrong about that?"

"I don't get your meaning."

"He just doesn't fit the profile. I expected him to look like a cold stone killer. He looks like the kids who write poetry at the coffee houses. He looks like he has parents who care for him, not some lone wolf terrorist hellbent on destroying good people. No question he was there and in Africa too. But I have to wonder why."

"You mean you don't recognize the face of pure evil? When they're good, you can't tell. You know this, Harper. You've seen it before. By looking like a college kid, he's adopted the perfect cover. Easy for him to pick up girls he could convince to help him. He gets to play the hero in a messed up, evil show."

"Lydia was expert at reading people. And I don't think she caught on, either."

"Don't think about it. She didn't have any reason to think something like that could even be possible. She's an innocent. Now you get to find out why, not to punish yourself, but to help us make sure it doesn't happen to other innocents."

Harper knew Patterson was right. And he was good with the direction. They'd started to become friends, even.

"One more thing before you go. I'd like a list and pictures of the aid workers that were supposed to be working there, when they started, and when they were to stop, plus what country they were from. You must have that because you talked about DNA of remains."

"I'm sure we have that. Anything else?"

"I want to know who the survivor was."

"Survivor? There weren't any."

"That's what I thought too. That's what I was told when they came to the house with the box. But then, who took the picture of the guy holding Lydia? You told me it was a survivor. Where did that picture come from? It wasn't on Lydia's camera. And how come it got brought back to me with her washed and folded clothes? Someone took the time to locate her cell, not to erase it, but to send it back to her family. Who would do such a thing?"

"I have no idea, Harper. But it's a mystery we better get solved ASAP. Someone out there knows something, and we have to find them."

"Unless someone in the group is trying to help us. Could that be possible?"

Patterson paused and then added. "I'm going to tell you what my old man used to tell me all the time growing up. 'Jerry, you ain't that lucky.'"

"That's funny. Your dad was a funny man."

"He was a son-of-a-bitch, but the Navy got me out of the house. If that's everything, I'm going to get started on that list and the pictures."

"Make sure you get their job descriptions too."

"Will do. You sound nervous, Harper. This stuff got you spooked?"

"Honestly, I took out a guy I was told was responsible for Lydia's death. Even though he was guilty of far worse, I don't want to do that again. I just want to get it right. No mistakes this time."

"Roger that. An admirable goal, Harper. Talk to you later on tonight perhaps."

"Will do."

He sent an email to Sally, asking her to send a copy of the DVD digitally to the admiral, and gave his email address. He told her he'd tell her all about it when he returned.

"Give Venom a hug and a steak from me," he ended his message with.

Harper heard the others getting up, taking showers, and making coffee. He wasn't going to say anything just yet, not until he figured out some of the holes in the story and questions he had. But something really wasn't adding up. Could there be somebody in the State Department or the police force who was in on the raid? Somebody who was trying to steer or protect someone else or even possibly protect Lydia and it backfired. He needed to check out every single lead before he could go further. And he was glad they apparently had the time to do so.

Shortly before noon, Lipori and four of his group piled into a Jeep and headed toward Imprunetta. A minute later, the three remaining men followed in a battered pickup truck painted with the logo for the olive farm. Harper had his guys split up, leaving two people behind making surveillance videos of anybody who arrived or stayed behind or staff that arrived during the day. Harper and two others would go into town, following the Jeep and the pickup.

He threw down some cereal and yogurt, took a cup of coffee and a banana, and slid behind the wheel of the rented Land Rover. On their way, he informed the guys in the apartment downtown of their plans. They arranged to meet in town at an espresso bar they had passed earlier. It would give them cover to just sip their cappuccinos and people watch.

He kept a safe distance to avoid being detected. Then he parked in a library parking lot two blocks away from the office building parking lot that both their vehicles drove into.

On the outside of the building, in Italian, were huge letters. "District of Florence Police Department."

"Probably not a good idea to break in there for a peek," Sean whispered.

Harper had an idea. "Look, you guys go downtown and get me a cappuccino. Bring everyone back here. I'll stay behind and take shots, and I'll let you know if I see anything. You'll be only about five minutes away. Okay?"

"If you go by those little shops, Harper, pick up some good Italian chocolate, okay? It will greatly enhance my sex life when I get back home."

"You have yourself a deal, Sam. And make mine a double."

CHAPTER 14

HARPER WAITED IN a phone booth, pretending to be on a call. It was warmer inside the little blue box, mostly because it protected him from the breeze.

He'd forgotten how many church chimes there were in Italy and all over Europe. But while Florence was known for the beautiful cathedrals, these little villages had tiny ornate chapels everywhere, all with bells announcing services. There were several shops in a line, all decorated with colorful canvas awnings, running down the street to the stop sign. He noticed a grocer next to a bakery, so he headed that way.

The next street over ended in a roundabout. In the center of the curbed island was a street vendor, selling fresh vegetables and flowers. There were so many colorful bouquets, they nearly looked like they were growing right out of the bed and windows of the old delivery truck holding them. He spotted some fresh ripe tomatoes, which were always good in Italy. In fact, all food was best in Italy, Harper thought. The vendor had baked goods as well.

He changed course and headed for the vendor, carefully dodging the speeding little cars buzzing around the circle like gnats.

He turned to check the front doors of the police station, noted the two vehicles still parked where Lipori's group left them, and found nothing remarkable.

As he swung back to face the vendor's cart, he was confronted with a huge bouquet of gloriosa daisies in a red plastic bucket, carried by a woman with dark hair. They nearly collided.

As she pushed her wares to the side, set the bucket down near his feet, and stood, brushing the hair from her forehead, Harper found himself face-to-face with Lydia.

At first, he couldn't speak. She started to frown, and it deepened when he said, "Lydia?"

Keeping her eyes on him, she shook her head. "I'm Georgie."

Her voice bore a slight Italian accent, but her English was perfectly spoken.

"Georgie?" he asked incredulously.

"Yes, sir. You are a tourist, an American?"

"I'm—I'm your husband."

She threw her head back and laughed. The syrup of

her sweetness engulfed him, as his heart noted how much he'd missed that lilting laughter, the soft white skin of her neck and the underside of her chin, and the way her hair flew back, her eyes filled with mirth as she stared up at the blue sky.

"Trust me, if I were your wife, I'd know it." Then she got serious. "You *are* joking, right?"

"Swear to God. No. We've been married five years. We lived in California where we met. You're a nurse. I lost you in Benin in West Africa while doing a mission with Doctors Africa. That was two years ago. We had a funeral—I have pictures of it I can show you."

She glanced behind Harper. "Look, my friend is coming, and I cannot talk about this. I think you're wrong, but I'd like to speak privately. But not now."

"Fine. When—"

"Georgie, someone else has been captured by your beauty?" asked a male voice behind him.

Harper saw her fear turn to a smile of greeting. But it wasn't for Harper. It was for the gentleman behind him. And, for the second time today, he was shocked to see who it was: Jakob Lipori, in the flesh.

"How do you do, Stranger. I'm Jakob." He stuck out his hand.

Harper had been trained to be wary, especially in shaking hands with known terrorists as there were many ways a lethal dose of poison could be exchanged that way. Harper coughed into his hands and then shrugged. "I'm sorry, but I have a cold. I best not shake hands. But it's nice to meet you." He nodded, rubbing his palms together, trying to appear contrite. He got a distrusting glare from Lipori.

"Georgie, you know this man?" he asked her without taking his eyes from Harper's.

For an instant, fear flashed across her face. Then she ran over to him and allowed his arms to encircle her. "You are so silly and too jealous. I've never seen him before, so stop teasing me, Jakob. You're not being polite."

"I think it's time we went home," he answered, leaning in for a kiss he did not land.

"I barely got set up. Let me stay an hour or two longer."

"We don't need the money today. Come. I'll help you pick everything up."

"I'm so sorry," interrupted Harper. "Apparently, I've caused something I didn't intend. She was just going to sell me some of those." He pointed to the gloriosa daisies in the bucket at his feet. "They are my girlfriend's favorite flower, and she'd be delighted. Please, I must insist. You totally misunderstand me, sir."

"See what you've done, Jakob? You've ruined my first sale of the day. Now go away and leave me alone.

This is my business. I'll be home by three."

Lipori didn't like the situation and stood close by, protectively guarding the space between Harper and the woman called Georgie. Harper was sure she was his wife. But was she also a wife or partner of Lipori as well? And how could all this have happened?

Whistles came from the direction of the truck and car. Harper turned to see Lipori's men standing nearby, waiting for him.

"I've got to talk to them. Georgie, do your transaction, and I'll be right over in a minute to help you close up." To Harper, he focused his dark eyes and, without a smile, added, "Thank you for your business." He jogged to the little gathering of men he came with. They took off in the truck, leaving Lipori behind with the car.

Lydia quickly wrapped the daisies in newspapers, stapling them secure, and handed him the bouquet.

"Ten U.S. dollars please. I assume you have this?"

"Yes, I do." Holding the bouquet in the crook of his elbow with his left arm, he reached into his jacket vest pocket for his wallet and produced the ten. He also passed to her a card with his phone number on it. "Just let me know when."

"Anything else you like?" she asked, taking the money and the card, putting it in her pocket.

He didn't want to end the conversation, and apparently, she didn't either. They were limited to speaking about the bright red tomatoes he loved, and he pointed to the loaf of bread when she told him she'd baked it herself last night.

She put everything in a plastic bag, carefully handling the tomatoes, nearly bursting with ripeness. He wanted to take her hand, to pull her aside and kiss her. He was desperate to continue the encounter, but Lipori was upon them in a flash.

"My goodness, you've nearly cleaned her out. She's famous for her tomatoes. You must love them."

"When in Italy, you know how it goes. Caprese salads are my favorite." It was the truth, but he still felt dumb admitting it. Adjusting the bag and still holding on to the bouquet, he nodded to both of them. "It was nice to meet you. I'm only here for a couple of days, so perhaps we'll meet again, but perhaps not. Thank you for these!" he said, holding up the bag.

"You need any help?" Lipori asked. Behind him, Lydia was putting boxes of vegetables and buckets of flowers away in the truck.

"I'm just a few blocks away," Harper lied. "I need the exercise." He took off in the direction of the corner. With his back turned to Lipori and Lydia, he placed his finger to his lips when he saw his Teammates drive slowly by with his cappuccino.

After he turned the corner, the car met him after

they'd rounded the whole block. He had not seen Lipori's men anywhere, but he kept looking.

Hamish was the driver. "We got your double. How come you walked right past us?"

"As you can see, Hamish, I have my hands full. Did you notice the cart in the roundabout?"

"A woman and a man. I saw them," said Sam, sitting next to Hamish and holding Harper's coffee. "And by the way, you're fuckin' welcome." He stuck his arm out in front of Hamish, through the open window.

Hamish wasn't liking the arm in the face. "Dammit, Sam. Let me have that. What's he going to do, balance it on the top of his head?"

Sam began a retort until Harper interrupted him.

"I saw Lydia. She was over at the vegetable and flower cart." He yelled, "Don't!" when Sam started to get out of the front seat.

"No way. You sure?" Hamish asked.

Harper slid behind him in the second seat, set the bag and flowers down on the seat, and grabbed his cold cappuccino. "You guys stop for lunch somewhere?"

"No, the other guys are at the coffee house," yelled Sam over his shoulder. "Explain, Harper, because I'm awfully confused."

"That makes two of us. Now, turn around without coming around the corner, and head back in the opposite direction. Don't turn around to look, but watch to make sure we aren't being followed."

"You sure it was her?" Hamish asked again.

"Would you recognize your wife if you didn't see her for two years? Would you have recognized her in a crowd after your first date?"

"Point taken. So what are we doing? Where are his other men?"

"We drop in on the dudes and then go home. I need to see if she lives at the villa or not. You didn't happen to shoot a picture, either of you?"

"Sorry, Boss," said Sam.

"Probably the best. But to answer your question, she claims not to be Lydia, and that was before Lipori came over."

"You talked to Lipori too?" gasped Sam.

"Yes. It appears she calls herself Georgie now, and I can't help but notice how possessive he is with her. I'd have to be an idiot not to see that they're together."

"No fuckin' way," Hamish said as he pulled into a parking spot in front of the coffee shop.

"Does that mean we consider her a terrorist now?" asked Sam.

Harper's insides were caving. That was an impossible thought, but what he'd just witnessed changed everything. He'd prayed every day to be able to just see her one more time. And now that he had, instead of pure joy, he felt nothing but dread.

Was he about to lose her again, this time to another man?

CHAPTER 15

A FULL MANIFEST was waiting for Harper on his computer when he returned to the villa. He scanned the list of names. He saw Lydia's name added to the bottom, which had probably been because they'd identified her remains last. He accounted for all the nurses and doctors. But he saw no mention of a teacher, which verified Harper's suggestions.

So Lydia did know her killer, or the man they thought had killed her. And why was her DNA identified and here if she was walking around, fully alive? And if she wasn't the one in the photograph, whose body was retrieved from the burn pit and sent home for the funeral?

But the biggest problem was the issue of why she'd taken up with Lipori—why she was even friends with a terrorist. It was impossible for Harper to grasp. He knew her; he knew everything about her. They shamelessly shared no secrets, except very private secrets they revealed and whispered to each other every time they made love. There was no way he could accept she didn't love him. And if she did, how could she have ever forgiven herself to move on? Did she have a twin adopted out she never known about? These things were not real.

None of it made any sense.

His bullshit meter was stuck smack dab between empty and full. He was delighted she was alive but deflated because she didn't appear to be free to rekindle what they had. He'd never considered that to be an outcome. All his planning had been about the mission to snatch Lipori and get him confined to a cell forever, if he was prohibited from sending him to the Source.

He hoped she'd take his card and call him. But could he trust her? What if she would tell Lipori who he was, do something to show her loyalty was now with Lipori and his men, his dirty deeds?

That was just impossible to accept.

He picked up the daisy bouquet. They had been her favorites. He hadn't lied about that. He still kept huge clumps of them growing in his house in Santa Rosa, all generated from the seeds she'd saved and lovingly labeled, tucked away in a small envelope. He'd used them sparingly, but having those daisies made him feel they were communicating through the grave.

He ran downstairs and found a large flower vase, filled it with water, and unwrapped the flowers. He found kitchen scissors and clipped off the bottom inch of stem and leaves, picked them up in clumps, and inserted them in their new home.

As he added the last clump, a yellow lined piece of paper was stuck to the underside, folded.

It was a number. Next to it, she'd written, "Text me first." And then she wrote her name, except it wasn't the name he'd whispered to her in bed. It wasn't the name of the person who wore those slippers still waiting for her tiny feet on her side of the bed, the name on her flowered water glass in the bathroom, or the name he thought of when he fell asleep on her pillow.

She'd written Georgie.

He looked at the printed list he'd been sent of the fatalities. There was a nurse on the manifest, G. Lemieux from Belgium. Could that have been a Georgie? But why would she take that name, except to hide her involvement in the massacre?

Could her body wounds be staged? The way her head hung backwards, her arms and legs limp, looked every bit like a dead body to Harper. If that was the nurse from Belgium, where had Lydia gone? And why was her DNA found in the firepit?

That photo was Lydia. He was sure of it. And Lipori was certainly the man who carried her to the car.

He had to talk to her. She had keys to the mystery she didn't realize she had. Only she could clear up those things. Depending on how it turned out, what they did with Lipori was different in every scenario he could think of.

He dialed Patterson and explained the encounter.

"That just can't be," the admiral said.

"I'm questioning your intel. Who was it who survived? Who took that picture, and who helped create the report? Am I looking for someone who is a terrorist or someone in our own government who is working for the other side?"

"That's the one scenario I don't want to know about, can't believe in," Patterson said.

"Why? Where's our proof? I need to know these things, because if we have someone working on the inside, she's in danger, and for that matter, so are all of us. Admiral, you have to help us out here. I can snatch Lipori today, but if he understands what we know, the stakes just went up tenfold."

"I completely agree, Harper."

"What about the president and his circle?"

"He's been pressuring me for information."

"Someone around him then?"

"As a former SEAL, you think he could be that gullible? I have a hard time buying that."

"Someone he trusts. It would explain a lot. Someone on the inside."

"I feel an obligation to explain it to him, but like you said, we need to know who helped create the report with the DNA results, the pictures."

"So can you trust him? Is that intel only he has, or

where did it come from?"

"I've tried to put out feelers. I just don't have an answer yet. I need a day. I'll circle back before I have to talk to him. In the meantime, try to get hold of her. See if she can give us any clues. I want to think she's somehow not involved, but, Harper, if she is, I can't protect her, and you better not either."

"Understood. This afternoon was one helluva of a find. Now we have to discover how it happened."

"I'll reach out to my Italian Special Forces guy too. Maybe you two should meet as well."

"I'm willing."

"Let me see if I can arrange it. How are the men?"

"Bored to death. I think that's about to change. You know how it is, the worse it gets the happier they are. I'd be the same way, except we're talking about the love of my life, my forever woman I was sure was lost. And now she's back in my life. Dangerously, back in my life. Admiral, you have to help me here. I can't lose her again."

Harper was notified that Lydia's truck had just driven up to the villa, followed by a car containing Lipori. He excused himself from the phone call to check in with the guys he'd left behind.

"Did others go and come this afternoon? What was the traffic?"

"A team of housekeepers descended on the villa right after you left. They worked about two hours then left with their equipment. We got the license plates if you want to look into them. Also, the guys who left returned with a policeman while they were having the house cleaned. The Civil Guard left before you got home."

Carl had given him a great report, and Harper thanked him.

"Let's call a meeting. Carl. Get the boys from town to come in too. You continue to keep an eye on that villa."

"Roger that. I'll be right back."

"You got pictures of the arrivals and departures, the Guard license plates?"

"I did."

"After you notify the guys, upload them here, and tell the admiral I said to send them. Explain what he's seeing in the photos." He gave Carl the admiral's card with his personal cell and secure email address.

"On it."

WITHIN MINUTES, THE team assembled in the living room. As requested, the men in town brought some fresh panini and drinks.

"We have a new development, and I want you to know where we're at, just so you are properly prepared."

Harper looked over the faces of his men, men he trusted with his own life.

"While we were tailing Lipori and several of his

guys, I had a random encounter with Lydia, my wife, the lady I was told had perished at the hands of Jakob Lipori, who lives here. I even met Lipori as well. They might suspect me, but we're getting things checked out before we act."

The room gasped, waiting for an explanation.

"She denied that she was Lydia, but there's no question she's under Lipori's control. He intervened, and I'm trying to make contact with her to get some answers. In my gut, I don't feel she's involved. I'm still thinking she's a victim. But I don't know for sure. So part of our mission will be to capture her as well and bring her back to the states. If she doesn't cooperate with me, it will be left to the State Department handlers, and you know how that works. But she's now, until we learn otherwise, part of the terrorist group."

It was complete silence.

"Why are we waiting then?" asked Knute. "Either way, she's coming with us. Biggest danger is that the bad guys smell a plan in the works and disappear before we can nab them. Shouldn't we be readying ourselves to go do that?"

"Yes, it is, and we will. I want to have one conversation with her, if I can."

"Harper, what if she'd tip them off? You have to be thinking of that as a possibility," said Paul.

"Which is why I want you to be ready, even for tonight. Once it's dark, that's always the best time. We also may have someone in D.C. or State we can't trust. Patterson is checking on a witness. None of you are to relay anything to anyone if you call home, understand? We're trying to figure out if we're being compromised in some fashion. That doesn't change the mission, just how we do it."

"What did she say when you talked to her? Did she have an explanation?" asked Sam.

Harper swallowed hard. It was hard to tell them this.

"She either doesn't remember me or is a very good actress and very dangerous. Let me also remind you, no harm is to befall any of those guys on Lipori's team. This isn't a kill mission, unless they're trying to use lethal force against you. I need to make sure you understand that."

The team, one by one, agreed.

He was ready to call the meeting. But Lydia did that for him. On his cell, he recognized the number from her paper. Her text was simple.

"Meet me at Angelo's Deli, thirty minutes. Come alone."

CHAPTER 16

"**I** AGREED TO meet you because you look like an honest man," Lydia said, sipping her coffee. Unlike Harper's cappuccino, she had ordered a chai latte with nutmeg. She noticed him staring down at it after she took the sip.

"Something wrong?" she asked.

"You never used to order that. We both ordered extra cream cappuccinos." He held out his drink. "Here, you try this and tell me it isn't divine."

She refused, crossing her arms and leaning back into her chair. "You've got to stop this, Mr. Cunningham."

That hurt.

"You still don't believe me? You don't think I don't remember every day we were married?"

"Let's go one step at a time. No. I don't believe you. How could I? I am a different person than you think you know. If you want to have a conversation with me, you've got to quit trying to 'win me over' with some garbage about your dead wife."

"And yet you agreed to meet with me. Explain this, please, because I didn't come here just to walk away and think I'd made a mistake. Somewhere—"

She stood up. "I can see this was an error."

Harper stood as well and grabbed her upper arm to turn her around. She glared at him, so he dropped his hand. "I'm sorry. I won't speak about it if you'll answer some questions I have. Believe me, L-L—Georgie, if I'm wrong, I'll apologize and go away. I will. But I need to find out a few things first."

He knew when she found out what his plans were for packaging and shipping Lipori to the U.S., he risked losing her for good. But it was worth it to get more clues as to what happened.

For a second, she looked resigned and sat. She checked her watch.

"I rescheduled an appointment to meet you. I can't stay long."

"So I'll make it quick. Who is Jakob Lipori to you? How did you meet him?"

She sipped her chai and stared into her lap. Her eyes wandered through the deli, searching the tables sparsely filled with locals. Outside, it had begun to rain. Then they made eye contact.

"I woke up in a hospital here, well, in Florence.

They told me I'd been involved in an accident. I'd apparently been in a coma for several months and wasn't expected to live."

She pulled aside the front of her shirt and revealed a large scar over her left side. It resembled post-surgical heart transplant photos he'd seen. Several bubble gum scars surrounded the massive area of scar tissue. A long thin line extended along her clavicle, heading out to her shoulder area.

Her eyes defiantly watched him take it all in. He couldn't help the tears that collected in his eyes, one spilling over. The massive scar tissue did speak to some heavy life-saving procedures done on her. He was grateful to whomever was responsible for her care.

Her expression softened slightly. She pulled back her shirt and then covered it with her jacket. "Do you believe that?"

"Of course I do." He reached into his pocket and produced the picture of her lifeless body being carried by a man that day in Africa. "This is what I was shown, as the proof of your death. Until then, I was given a report of an aid mission in Benin that went horribly wrong, where a group of terrorists murdered the missionaries, you among them. I knew you to be a nurse. I was to follow you there, but you were gone before I could make it."

Her expression was hard to read. Her forefinger

brushed against the image of the man who carried her. He needed to be careful, but he had to ask the question anyway.

"Do you believe me?"

She hesitated, reflex starting to kick in to deny what her eyes were seeing "I was told another story, and photographs can be altered."

Harper knew this had to be the case and was glad she was finally willing to talk about how she got here.

"I believe you. Some important people I trust with my life say no. You know who that man is, don't you?"

She refused to answer.

"Okay then, tell me about your life here and how you met Jakob Lipori?"

"You would have me believe he's a terrorist?"

"Do you love him?"

Again, her eyes went to flame. "How dare you—"

"It's a simple question. I need to know. Are you in love with him? Think about it carefully because your answer has consequences."

"Are you a policeman, CIA agent?"

"No. I am not. But I've been searching for you for these past two years, and even though asked to give up, I've refused." He knew it was a little white lie. He'd believed she was dead and didn't hope to believe she still might be alive. But he had to make it fit into what could be plausible, and he had to go carefully since he could see there was a relationship there.

"I'm not into revenge, if that's your idea of getting acquainted with me. Trying to dirty the man I live with."

"You live with him, but do you love him?"

"I owe him a great deal—"

"The question still stands."

"What are you looking for?"

Fair enough. "I'm looking for my wife. Search yourself, and see if you think she's in there," he pointed to her heart.

Her eyes welled over.

"I don't mean you any harm. Honest. I just need to know."

"I had lost all of my memory when I woke up. They said it would come back in months' time, but it never has. I've had flashes of things that don't make any sense. I wanted to do research, see if I could find if I had a family. I was told the research came up empty, no matches. Seems that I'm a one of a kind."

"Impossible. Who told you that?"

"Jakob."

"And you gave him the vials after you were tested, or the swabs, or whatever?"

"The hospital did it."

"And he arranged it."

She stared at her lap and nodded. Tears were

streaming down her cheeks. Harper wanted to take her in his arms and reassure her, but that was risking more than he could afford.

"You have a sister in Seattle and two nephews who used to call me all the time and ask me if I was okay. You have co-workers at the hospital you worked at. People who knew you from the group of health professionals who helped to tend to victims of floods, natural disasters, and war in third world countries. They all miss and love you. Everyone knows you as Lydia. My wife."

She looked up at him in pain. He reached over and grasped one of her hands on the table. "We were very much in love. See if you can find any of that there. Focus on it."

She withdrew her hand, tired, confused, and fearful.

"Jakob paid for my care. He is responsible for my life. He agreed to help me find my family, and when he couldn't find anyone, he gave me a place to live, gave me something I loved doing. I never knew anything about nursing. I hate the sight of blood and nearly faint when I see it."

"No wonder." He tapped the picture, showing the huge stain covering most of her chest. "So you enjoy being a street vendor? Or do you do something else?"

"I teach gardening classes. I love to garden—it's the

first thing I started doing when I recovered that seemed to make me feel whole. Until then, I was going crazy, searching for bad guys in crowds and looking for someone close by who wanted to kill me."

A tiny flicker of fire began to spread, warming his wounded heart. She had gotten in touch with one of her loves. Now, if he could somehow get her to remember another—if he had time. Maybe she never would. He had to face that fact.

"I understand. That would be horrible, wake up and not know who you are. How did you get your name?"

"The hospital said they found something on me. A wristband or something. Anyway, this all happened here in Italy. Not in Africa. I've never been to Africa."

"Oh, but you have," he said, again tapping on the picture. "And you know who that is. So now tell me, what is the truth, hmm?"

"But why would he be so good to me? Pay for all those surgeries, stand by me through it all? He was kind. He's protective of me. His job is to keep me safe. You're asking me to distrust someone who has been keeping me safe now for months. He's selfless."

Harper considered several things. He could go either way. He had some photographs he could show her, but she could easily discount them as not belonging to what Jakob really did in life. He could ask a bunch of questions about him and what he did with his time while she was working in her garden. But would she accept it or go running back to his arms. If that happened, they'd disappear forever, especially if she told him what Harper had revealed about their marriage.

He decided on another tactic.

"When I met you at the cart, you asked me not to talk about knowing you from the past in front of Jakob. Why did you do that?"

"You're an American. I asked you that, remember? I guess just a romantic idea of Americans, since I was told I must have been raised there. They guessed I was here on holiday when the accident happened."

"What accident?"

"The auto accident. I hit a truck with a load of rebar in the back, and several pieces came through the windshield and pinned me. Nicked my heart. Jakob paid for a transplant after I was stabilized. My heart was healed but still significantly damaged. It was going to fail."

"How did you get those round fleshy scars to the side?"

She reached into her blouse and let her fingers run over the scars. He could see she was circling the edges with her forefinger, lost in thought.

"The rebar."

"No, ma'am. Those are gunshot wounds. Close range, probably a .22. You were lucky it was low caliber."

Her eyes grew wide. "No, that—"

Harper leaned over the table. "Listen to me carefully. You're in danger. I'll call you whatever you like. I won't make any demands on you, but please pay attention. You cannot trust Jakob Lipori. I don't know why he saved you, but he must have. I have been told by others, but again, I wasn't there, that he was partially responsible for the massacre that day and has been identified as your shooter."

He let that sink in. He knew it was a bitter pill. He deduced she was running it all through her bullshit detector. She was still loyal, a trait she'd possessed in spades. She cared about life and pretty things. It wasn't everything, but he could see she was still partially there. Lydia, some form of her, was still there.

If she'd let him, he'd devote the rest of his life trying to bring back the other parts. He was even willing to accept the consequences if he failed. But not another death. He would not allow that to occur, even if he lost her every other way.

But as long as she breathed, talked to him, let him tell her stories, somehow, he knew he could bring her fully back.

CHAPTER 17

H E WATCHED HER slip out to the street, place her jacket hood over her head, and scamper down the wet sidewalk and out of view. Harper waited for evidence of changes in the crowd of pedestrians or parked cars while he dialed the guys at the villa. He kept his focus when Hamish picked up his phone.

"How'd it go, Boss?"

"More on that later. I want you and two others to get back into town. I've directed her to enter the tourist shop near the police station in that little strip. I can't tail her, but I'm pretty sure she's in danger. Go in the rear entrance and get her out. You can take her to the apartment until I arrive."

"We're already there. Any requests?"

"Take one of the medics and Carl. I want him positioned in the upper window, looking out toward the plaza, okay?"

"We're on it."

He saw a brown Fiat with tinted windows, appearing to have two men in it, turn around and head in Lydia's direction.

Fuck!

He texted her, letting her know she was being followed, hoping she was nearly at the shop or already there. "My guys are on the way. Stay safe."

He got back a praying hands emoji in answer, unless someone else had obtained her phone. He was in the process of calling the admiral when he felt the cool steel of a gun barrel at the back of his head. Whoever it was remained unfazed by the curious stares from the customers, who began moving around, some going to the back rooms, others running out the front door.

"Lock it," he yelled before the next person could escape.

Harper knew that voice. He doubted he'd have the time to reach into his pants and grip his KA-BAR or pick out his Sig from the inside of his jacket vest pocket. So he did the next best thing. He raised both hands as if surrendering, bending his arms at the elbow, and then turned and struck the gun so fast it flew across the floor. He landed a roundhouse kick to Lipori's beautiful nose and watched it explode in a loud crunch, spewing blood in a twenty-foot arc.

Lipori lay on his back, choking on his own blood.

"I want to make a deal," Lipori said, suddenly looking about sixteen years old. Harper knew he'd probably been surprised he was old enough to be Lydia's father. He underestimated the SEAL to his own peril.

"No deals. Unless you want to return to the Source, and then I might grant you that wish. How about it, Jakob? You want to be a martyr? Or did your parents tell you communism could save your life?"

"They can pay."

"Thanks for that information," Harper said while he checked the outside. No sirens yet. One of the customers wanted to unlock the door and flee. "Not yet. Give me a minute or two, and you can go." He turned to the crowd. "You're all safe here. Just let me wrap up a few details, and you'll all be free to leave. And you'll lose your cell phone and get charged for helping a terrorist if I see anyone calling out."

Harper knew it wouldn't be a one hundred percent solution, but it was worth a try. He hauled the still sputtering Lipori to the corner away from the view of the glass front windows. On the way, he picked up Jakob's piece. It was a Glock, of course.

He stuck the gun in his pants waistband in the back.

He shoved Lipori down into the seat, nearly crushing the rickety chair. He called to one of the waiters, who had hidden behind the counter. "You there!" he yelled. Three people stood, with their hands in the air.

"First person who can give me a couple of strong zip ties gets to leave."

They looked at each other in shock.

"Go! If you value your life, get me those fuckin' zip ties."

All three stumbled over each other and got quickly into action.

His phone beeped, and he got the confirmation the boys had picked her up and were heading to the apartment. It would be close enough to walk, since he had no intention of driving the car, which probably had a tracking device on it.

Lipori's phone beeped with a message. Harper kept his Sig on his forehead, reaching into Jakob's jacket to grab the phone. He had no idea what he'd sent, but he clicked the alternative message. It was in Italian. Whatever it was, the party didn't call back. He turned off the phone but didn't destroy it. He might need some of his contact numbers.

His gamble had paid off. He'd told her about what he really did. He took a chance there was enough of Lydia there to pull her in his direction. Now he had to figure out how to get this asshole out of the shop quickly without notifying the local authorities.

An older waiter with a stained apron held out his fist clutching a half dozen heavy zip ties. Not only was his hand shaking, so was his whole arm. His face appeared to be in shock.

"Perfect! You want to leave?"

The waiter shook his head.

"Then get back there, and keep the kids calm. No one runs out, and no one tries to call anyone. If you get them to cooperate, everyone will be safe."

The older man with the salt and pepper moustache nodded his head repeatedly and retreated behind the counter.

Harper bound Lipori to the chair, which would make a running escape more difficult. He secured his ankles together and then stuck the additional ties in his pocket with Lipori's cell.

He called Hamish again. "Major thanks. Now I need an extraction. I knew there was a reason I had you come along. No one better at extractions than you, my friend."

"Are you okay? What's going on? We've got Lydia."

"Make sure you don't let her go, and you get over here to help me unload a package to the trunk."

"I'm on it."

"And, Hamish," he whispered out of earshot of Lipori. "I'm going to call in a raid on their villa. So ask the guys to be prepared to leave quickly and load up all the gear, just in case. Everyone's."

"Got it. I'm on my way. Do I call Patterson, or are you okay until I get there?" he asked, sounding like he was running.

"Nope, I'll get him. I just got to move this guy, and the trunk is the best place I can think of."

Lipori's phone rang again. Harper repeated the same message.

Hamish came through the back. "You got a mass exodus in the kitchen, Harper."

"Figures. The car back there?"

"Yup. Help me with this chair."

The two of them carried Lipori, who was objecting so loudly Hamish slapped him hard with the back of his hand. Lipori's head rolled forward unconscious.

"I can't stand whining. Some of these kids never learn that their actions have consequences. That's what's wrong with the modern generation."

Harper studied the puzzled faces of the customers and staff as they moved the terrorist and his throne to the trunk then shoved him in. Hamish got behind the wheel, ready to take off. Harper raised his finger after studying the alleyway for overly curious onlookers with a cell phone. He didn't see any. But he knew someone must have reported it.

He ran inside and announced. "Show's over, folks. This was a drill. Nothing to worry about. We do these things all the time. His nose will heal. Not to worry. Have a nice life."

Nobody moved at first. Then they piled up at the

doorway, struggling to get out in twos and threes. Of course, that also kept Lipori's buddies in the brown Fiat from being able to enter, as the customers exited like a herd of buffalo.

Harper took out Lipori's sim card, broke it in half, and tossed it out the window.

"Where to?"

"The apartment for now. You get hold of the boys at the villa?"

"On their way. Caesar says they got another busload of young males, and it appears they're clearing out the house. They're leaving, Harper."

"Wish we could have gathered their paperwork and computers. I'll let Patterson's guys worry about that."

"They'll probably torch it if they aren't coming back."

"Fine by me. His family owns it."

He called Admiral Patterson and let him know what was going on. He requested a quick extraction and was given the location of a small municipal airport about fifty miles away, toward the Italian Riviera. It was used for a flight school but was big enough to land larger jets in an emergency.

"We're coming in three groups. Sorry to say I'm leaving the Volvo in Imprunetta. It might have been placed with a tracking device. But everything else will be at the airstrip. The map came through perfect."

"I already sent it to your coms guy, Sam. I'll confirm you're on your way as well."

"Thanks."

The map he sent to Carl and the instructions to bring everything, including Lydia, was given a thumbs-up, plus the message, "She's a little scared, but on board. No worries there."

Harper responded, "Don't lose that lady. She means more to me than my own life." Hamish headed for the coordinates. Harper helped him check for Italian authorities, drank a bottle of water he grabbed from Hamish, and tried to relax.

But it was impossible. So much had happened today. So much could have gone very bad. So much still at risk.

But it was still a miracle.

CHAPTER 18

ON THE HIGHWAY toward the airport, they passed several patrol cars flying down the wet two-lane road. He followed them out the back of the car, and sure enough, a couple of miles back, where they had no guardrail, the cars did a U-turn and headed back toward them.

"They're turning back."

"I saw that," said Hamish. "We're not far. I see an alternate route, a little slower, but after we get over this swale, they won't see us turn off. Let the two behind us know about it, and have them slow down to let the police pass."

"I'm thinking you had bootleggers in your family, Hamish. You're skilled at avoiding police."

"You don't want to know. But you better get them the message right now."

Harper did so. Even described what was on the corner where they would turn.

Before long, the highway was hidden from view. They slowed down, due to the narrow road, and wandered through a semi-residential area until they came to another small freeway. In less than five minutes, they were outside the landing strip gates. Their transport was just arriving. They drove onto the tarmac as close as was safely possible.

Hamish unlocked the trunk and whistled to a crew member to help him with getting the prisoner onto the jet. Harper helped until he saw the other two cars drive up. The team began onboarding their equipment and personal items while Harper came around to the car and helped Lydia step out.

He wasn't going to push for a compliment or thank you. He imagined she was confused. He tried to ignore her but made sure she had help with a couple of items she'd brought from the apartment. The fuzzy blanket she had tightly wrapped around her body. She was shivering.

"Almost over now. Once we're in the air, you're safe."

"What will happen to Jakob?"

"We've got him restrained, but he's alive. He'll be going back with us. My job is done, and his disposition will be left to others."

She was standing close to him then looked up, just like she used to do, her brown eyes glistening, searching for meaning inside his soul. At last, she spoke.

"You're a brave man, Harper. I thank you for my life."

"No problem." He looked in the direction of the jet and saw they were being hailed. "We better get onboard. You have everything?"

"I do."

Out of reflex, he grabbed her hand and ran, pulling her along, careful not to have her stumble.

Hamish had his diapers in a twist. "Christ, you two. The whole world is at war, and you're acting like it's a fine summer day. You should hear the Navy pilot inside. He's going to have to change his pants when we get to Germany."

"We're going to Germany?" she asked.

"We'll get a transport to the east coast from there. Not sure when but hopefully tonight."

"I don't have my passport."

"You've got connections you never knew you had, Lydia," Harper said as he followed her inside. The crew closed the door. The jet did a taxi turn and then revved. In seconds, they were airborne.

Harper's team was high-fiving and regretting the fact that they'd not brought along some beer or fine Italian wine to celebrate. Lydia was getting nervous with all the bravado.

"Come on. I'll give you some privacy. Just a couple,

maybe three hours to go, but you can sleep in the rear. It's more quiet."

She got up, still wrapped in the blanket. He searched for and found some pillows, lowered arm rests in a row, placed the pillows down, and motioned for her to sit then lie down. He pulled the blanket loosely around her, added another, and carefully removed her shoes on those tiny feet of hers. She was wearing red nail polish. It made him chuckle.

"What's wrong?" she asked.

"You always wore red nail polish on your toes. So funny you would remember that."

"I didn't. I just chose. I like the color red."

He smiled gently down on her while sitting on the armrest across the aisle. "I know."

She rolled onto her back, pulling the blanket up to her chin. He brought down another pillow for her to set her feet on as she was slightly longer than the row of seats. He squeezed her feet, one at a time, but stopped there.

She was still watching him. "What will happen to me?"

"I don't know. You'll be held for interviews. Did you do anything you shouldn't have?"

She pulled her arm under her head to prop up slightly. "I got a speeding ticket and then forgot to show up for the court date. I ran over the neighbor's chicken, that foul old thing used to poop all over my car. One day, I left the hose running all day."

He couldn't get enough of her aura from where he sat. That she would even think these would be infractions amazed him. One thing he did notice was that she had become more docile. He remembered her being fearless, willing to take on challenges. He imagined with everything she had experienced both before and after her ordeal, she didn't trust herself. He didn't blame her for that.

"I think you'll be fine."

"What was I like?"

It almost brought tears to his eyes. "The best woman. The kindest, most beautiful woman I've ever met. You were the first one I really fell in love with. I used to think it would never happen to me."

"And then I was gone. It must have been hard for you."

He couldn't look her in the eyes when he answered, "You could say that." He checked on the guys up front, who had suddenly gotten quiet. He suspected many of them had retreated into their earbuds, playing their favorite music.

"Do you remember anything at all? You said you got glimpses, strange dreams. What did you dream about? Anything from your previous life? Our previous life? Did you recognize me at the cart?"

"I wish I could say I remembered you, your face, but I didn't, Harper. I'm sorry for that. I saw a lot of flowers in my dreams. It gave me the idea to start gardening. No one taught me. Maybe I remembered that from before. No one taught me to speak English, either, and yet I started talking just as soon as I was awake."

"They'll probably recommend hypnotherapy and other treatments. In time, you might remember some things. If it's been two-plus years, I doubt it will all come back."

"Where will you be?"

"I'll be in California with my team. Or up in Sonoma County at my house."

"Will I get to see it some day?"

He was literally shaking on the inside. It took everything he had not to do something inappropriate, like hug her so hard he'd knock her breath out.

"I'd like to show you. When they are through with you. And you do know they may need to hold you for a time. Lipori was a very high-level terrorist, causing the loss of life to many people during his reign. He associated with lots of other criminals and terrorists. He must have brought people by the villa. They might want help from you. Just consider this. Helping them get their answers will speed up the time when you can be cleared. I'll be available by phone, if it's allowed."

"You mean, unless I'm incarcerated."

"I can't promise that. Just like you wanting to remember, I can't lie and tell you I know how it's all going to work out. We'll take it one day at a time. But I'm not going anywhere. I just can't interfere with the process. You understand?"

She nodded. Her eyes were glazing over. He'd bored her to death. After she started snoring, he pulled the blanket under her chin and let her sleep.

Hamish stood, slapping Harper's back. "How you holding up?"

"You know me. Right as rain." He scanned his audience in front of him. Every set of eyes was studying his face. "Yeah, I admit it. I'm a bullshit liar."

THEY STAYED OVERNIGHT at the German air base and had tickets, first class even, leaving mid-day. The rest of their gear would be shipped through the military transport system, since their gear contained explosives and ammo and extra firepower.

They went to a beer pub frequented by U.S. Military and ordered some of that luscious German beer. Almost all of them got drunk, so they hired a taxi to go back to base, since they didn't want to be picked up for being drunk in public. Harper had a good buzz on, but he wouldn't have the hangover the others would.

He showered and stripped down to his boxers and

a t-shirt. He checked himself out in the mirror and wondered if he'd look younger if he shaved his beard or cut his hair. He was looking a little wild and wooly. He decided in the morning he'd look for a good barber and get cleaned up. Who knew? He might have to have another discussion with the president. Did he really go looking like this? The commander-in-chief must have thought he was a complete slob.

Patterson called. They'd found the leak. His confidential source was solid, but he had a son who was a leftie and had fallen into a group causing trouble. Patterson said it didn't appear the kid wanted to overthrow the world, but they used this useful idiot anyway. Harper had seen young boys over in Africa so afraid at what they were doing they peed themselves as they held people at gunpoint. In their mother's house one day and then out in the bush following a madman the next. He felt so very sorry for those boys and for those families who had lost their treasure.

He felt less sorry for the ones like Lipori. Patterson said his parents had taught political science at the University of Cologne and were avowed anarchists. That's how the kid picked it up. Who in their right mind would let their kid go off and do something like that? Yup, he thought, evil was a disease, not a condition.

"What's going to happen to Lydia?"

"I think she's going to be okay. Depends on how she cooperates."

"I gave her a little talk about that. She will, trust me."

"I have faith she'll be cleared. But it might take a few months."

"Where will she be?"

"Here in D.C.. She'll be housed and have a twenty-four hour female guard."

"Fun times. Will I be able to see her?"

"I think so. You are legally married."

"Oh, that's funny. Now you're being hilarious. You think that makes a difference since she won't let me touch her—not that I tried."

"I'd be surprised if you didn't try to bring out the woman who is still there, Harper. Don't discard this one. Don't do that to yourself."

"What happens if she doesn't want to see me, be around me? Never remembers who I am or what we meant to each other?"

"That's up to the doctors, Harper. My suggestion, for what it's worth, is to try. Try to convince her. I'd plan to visit on a regular basis."

"Except I'll be working, right?"

"You've earned some time off."

"Jeez, I was only hired for less than a month. I don't hardly call that work."

"You got the package. Everyone came home safe. No innocent loss of life. Yeah, we owe the rental company a couple of cars, but all in all, I'd say it was perfect. Now we're working on the whole program, filling out the prospectus. Soon, we'll get you involved. You might have to spend some time here in meetings. We're giving you time. You'll still get paid, and so will the men. We all know evil doesn't rest. There will be more, trust me. In the meantime, rest. Dream, and remember what it felt like to fall in love. All over again, if it takes that."

"Oh I never forgot that part. I think about it every night when I go to bed. Alone."

"A good place to start."

When he hung up, he heard a couple arguing in the room next door. The hotel was frequented by American GIs who took weekend leave and, with little pay, could only afford the strip-down motel they'd housed everyone in.

His phone rang.

"Harper? I'm sorry if I woke you," Lydia said.

"No, I was just turning in. Everything okay with you?"

"Yes. I sat for my first interview. Then my female guard took me shopping for some new clothes. I've lost so much weight my old clothes wouldn't fit me anymore."

"You more than earned the right to have new ones. I think that's perfect. Time for a fresh start, right?"

"Right. Remember when you asked me if I remembered anything? Well, I do."

Harper sat up, placing his feet on the floor.

"Tell me. That's great. What did you remember?"

"A dog. A big black dog. His name was Venom."

THREE MONTHS LATER

AFTER ALL THE meetings, the plannings with the task force President Collins had set up, which included several senators, Admiral Patterson, and other representatives from the CIA, FBI, and State Department, they were ready to launch Operation Silver Team.

Though Harper was part of the task force, along with his buddy Hamish McDougall, they were not going to be the public face of the Team, not while they were active. In fact, all the members of Silver Team, now increased to twenty-two, were to be kept secret from the general public for the safety of the team as well as the project.

Several priority hotspots and missions had been scheduled on a tentative basis. The Team still had to get the Defense Department's approval, plus final Senate Confirmation. Admiral Patterson would be the force's first director, which was a minimum four-year term, renewable at the discretion of the Senate or the

President of the United States. It was thought that, in this way, any attempts to make the appointment and running of this team a political "jewel in the crown" would fail if either body wished to approve, but it took both to agree to shut the department down.

However, Patterson had told Harper that nothing in Washington, D.C. was forever, and try as they might, everything was always politics, dealmaking. They were able to give security clearances to the Team members, as well as allow the operators to add to their military or other pensions, should they come from those departments.

They were greenlit, and members of the Team were given a well-deserved victory lap, being able to take turns staying in the White House one night of their choosing. Harper was pleased with all the accomplishments, save one.

Jakob Lipori was found guilty of terrorism, and a jurisdictional dispute arose shortly after his capture. President Collins refused to bow to U.N. pressure. The roundup and conviction of the group in Florence left behind was left to the Italians, and they made great headway with it. It was a story that ran for weeks in all the papers and on television.

But Lipori had been useful in giving names, even implicating his parents who had formed an insurrectionist club called "Democracy Live," a misnomer, which had spread throughout Europe. More than one European official was taking up the cause of rooting out terrorist roots. If it wasn't taken to extreme, Harper and Patterson both thought perhaps some permanent good could come of it.

But the U.S. claims to Lipori remained steadfast, and the creation of Silver Team was the envy of other nations who also wanted to tackle this issue and would be cooperating with the Team, even inviting them to help with issues in their own countries.

But the one part of this whole operation that hadn't been completed was his relationship with Lydia. Her memories were not coming back. He met with her nearly once a week, at least, but never without the security detail around her constantly. Dinners were not private. Conversations were recorded and also not private. She hadn't said so, but Harper thought they needed to change all that.

"To your place? You mean in California?" Patterson asked him.

"Yes, without the detail. I can get one of my guys to hang around, but don't you think you've put her through enough? She's been cleared. The investigation is complete, or that's what I was told. She's getting frustrated with the whole process and feels like a prisoner in her own country."

Patterson got permission. Harper asked her one

evening, in front of the agent, and Lydia was delighted.

"My therapist thought that if I went back to the place where I lived, it might help with the healing. No promises, Harper. He said there were no certain fixes, but it was worth a try, if I wanted to."

"And do you want to?" he'd asked her.

Her answer charmed him, just like everything else she did. She might not have realized it, but he would do anything she asked. Absolutely anything. He was glad she didn't demand he whisk her away and they live off the grid. He'd have done that.

"I do. I want to know about the Lydia I used to be."

"Then it's settled. Let's plan it, and let things go where they may," he'd whispered, because his voice was cracking like a schoolboy's.

They had taken walks together and held hands, and he'd hugged her, placed his arm around her shoulder to whisper things, and he felt her responding to him, but that was as far as it went. Nothing was promised about the home visit, but that would depend on Lydia. Harper would never push, although everything inside was screaming for a deeper, more intimate relationship. He felt he'd done everything he could to show his loyalty and his love for her without telling her so. He wanted to be able to hurdle the walls and get to show more how he felt for her. He wanted to share the experience with her, and if that miracle came where she shared back, well, life would turn out to be close to perfect.

TODAY WAS THE day of her arrival. Patterson had hired a driver to pick her up at the airport and bring her and her things to his place in Santa Rosa. When the driver left, they would be alone. Alone for the first time since she'd been rescued.

Venom was especially needy this day. Everywhere Harper went, the dog was right there next to him, looking closely at what he was working on, such that he kept getting in the way. Even using the bathroom, Harper had a loyal friend, as if he might need protection. Venom watched in front of the refrigerator as he put away the gourmet foods he'd bought for this special visit.

Harper talked to him about unloading the dishwasher, and Venom followed him from the machine to the cabinets or drawers as he was putting things away. He walked along Harper when he went outside to water the garden and pick big bold Gloriosa Daisies for the table, just like she'd always done for him when she lived there.

Sally offered to take Venom, but Harper refused. He wouldn't want to rob the dog's reunion with her. He couldn't wait to see his reaction.

He got a notice and picture on his phone of the

black town car coming up the driveway. He scanned his living room and then outside to the garden, through freshly cleaned windows. Everything looked perfect and ready.

The gravel driveway noisily announced them. He stood at his front door, Venom sitting at his side.

When the driver opened Lydia's door, and she stepped out, Venom gave a howl but stayed put. He looked up to Harper, asking permission to go to her, but Harper restrained him.

"She doesn't know you yet, Venom. Give her time."

But she messed up his command of the dog. She bent over and called him. This time, Venom didn't even check with Harper but bolted straight for her. He completely pushed aside the driver, who had his hands full of luggage and bags and nearly toppled.

The dog waited with anticipation, sitting erect right in front of her. As she petted the top of his shiny black head, he gave a moan, a long, tearful moan.

"What a good boy, Venom. Mama missed you."

It was what she used to tell him. Was it something she'd learned or something she recalled? Either way, it gave Harper a thrill that warmed his whole body.

She was fussing over the dog, letting him lick her face, playing with his ears and stroking the sides of his face. Harper gave instructions to the driver to leave the luggage inside the door and made his way over to Lydia.

"Welcome. I've waited so long for this day."

"As have I," she said, leaning over and giving him a kiss on the cheek. It had embarrassed her.

"Does any of this look familiar?"

"I recognize Venom. Do you by chance raise flowers?" she asked.

"Of course. I'll show you." He took her hand without asking permission and passed the driver on his way back to the car.

"Thanks," she said, waving.

"No problem, Ma'am. You have my card in case you'll be needing anything additional. Thank you, Mr. Cunningham."

He led her through the doorway and let go of her hand so she could wander. She noticed the flowers on the table right away and smiled up at him. "You grew these?"

"I did. You taught me. They're from seeds you saved when you lived here."

He was thinking how the room began to glow, just like it had done when she lived there. He noticed right away how the whole world seemed brighter, happier, now that they were in the presence of some kind of magic. Their chemistry was still there, bare and unprotected, intimate, yet they'd barely touched. He was hoping she was feeling the same. But he'd told himself he'd give her all the time in the world. And he wanted her to come to him, not the other way around. It had to be that way.

"I do feel like I know this place," she said, turning around, walking over to the piano, some of the antiques that they bought together and others he got from his mother.

"You'll want to check out the garden," he said, pointing to the glass doors leading out to the deck and garden area. He noticed how the Gloriosa Daisies outside reflected into the room and turned everything golden.

She slid open the door and stood halfway in and halfway out, facing his flower garden.

"Harper!" And then she was quiet.

"Yes?" he whispered into her ear. "What is it?"

"I—I…" She turned to face him. He was still bent over, so very close. Her eyes searched his. Did she see the tears he had for her? Did she see it? He wanted her to. Focusing on his lips, she said, "I remember this."

He didn't think his heart could take any more. But he was wrong.

She slid her hands up under his ears and pulled his mouth close and then onto hers, while she plied her softness against his need, taking his breath away. Carefully, he slipped his arm around her waist and pulled her to him, brought her against him, feeling her heart beat as they kissed, fulfilling the dream he'd had so many times.

He was no longer worried that she saw his tears.

She had them too. They faced each other, staring and letting the moment wash over them both, their breathing ragged.

Venom stirred up attention as he took off chasing a squirrel. They both laughed.

"Come. I'll show you," he said, taking her hand again, but kissing the top of it first before leading her past the flower boxes, past the rows of cabbage, broccoli, lettuce, and his tomato trees. "They're not as nice as the ones you grew."

"They look wonderful. Everything looks wonderful. Did we—?"

He smiled.

"Did we do this together?"

"What do you think? Close your eyes and see us there. Do you see it?"

She had closed her eyes and smiled, her face upturned to his. Waiting.

He whispered to her lips, "We did lots of things in the garden." He gave her a gentle kiss. "I'd love to show you everything, Lydia. Do you see it?"

"I feel it. I want you to show me, Harper. Show it all to me. Bring it all back. I want it all."

IT WAS MIDNIGHT when he awoke. She was lying in his arms, just like they used to do, her head on her pillow which he'd finally washed. His fingers lazily laced up and down her spine until she began to stir and respond, kissing his neck and pressing her upper torso into his with her arms wrapped around him.

"I can see it will be a beautiful life, Harper. And if it all doesn't come back, we'll make more memories, right?"

"Absolutely."

She slid closer, but her leg got caught on Venom's hard body. The dog had wedged himself between them.

"Off, Venom," he said, and Venom at first refused, then jumped off the bed, and left the room.

"That might take me a bit to get used to."

"He loves you, Lydia," he said as he accepted her kisses. She was climbing on top of him, showering him with her scent, her hair, the view of her naked body making him ache for her again, but this time, he knew his pain would be eased, and he'd have her all over again.

He held her head as she kissed him. "As do I, Lydia. Forever and forever."

"Me too, Harper. In fact, I think I loved you even before I realized it. But this is better."

"Much better."

"Let's start the day every day like this."

He flipped her onto her back. "It's a deal. I promise."

Did you enjoy Something About Silver?

You can followup with Harper and Lydia in the next
book in this series:

Loving Harper

Which is in Lydia's POV as they come together closer
And battle the bad guys.

Want more SEALs?

To read the original SEAL Brotherhood Series, either
start with

Accidental SEAL

Or if you know you want them all try

Ultimate SEAL Collection #1 or

Ultimate SEAL Collection #2

Other SEAL Series:

SEAL Brotherhood: Legacy

Bad Boys of SEAL Team 3

Band of Bachelors

Bone Frog Brotherhood

Bone Frog Bachelor

Sunset SEALs

You can always get any of my upcoming books,
Sharon's other pen names and information on
my website:

Sharonhamiltonauthor.com

ABOUT THE AUTHOR

 NYT and USA/Today Bestselling Author Sharon Hamilton's SEAL Brotherhood series have earned her author rankings of #1 in Romantic Suspense, Military Romance and Contemporary Romance. Her other *Brotherhood* stand-alone series are: Bad Boys of SEAL Team 3, Band of Bachelors, True Blue SEALs, Nashville SEALs, Bone Frog Brotherhood, Sunset SEALs, Bone Frog Bachelor Series, SEAL Brotherhood Legacy Series and SEAL Brotherhood: Silver Team. She is a contributing author to the very popular Shadow SEALs multi-author series.

Her SEALs and former SEALs have invested in two wineries, a lavender farm and a brewery in Sonoma County, which have become part of the new stories. They also have expanded to include Veteran-benefit projects on the Florida Gulf Coast, as well as projects in Africa and the Maldives. One of the SEAL wives has even launched her own women's fiction series under the pen name of Annie Carr. But old characters, as well as children of these SEAL heroes keep returning to all the newer books.

Under the pen name S. Hamil, she has a new Dystopian/Sci-Fi/Fantasy Romance, Free to Love. Book 1 of this 5-book series has been released: Free As A Bird. The story arc is about a future alternative universe where Androids are feared because of their AI capabilities that outpace human intelligence, and yet the hero, an android, may become the savior of the world, both human and other.

Annie Carr, Sharon's Women's Fiction author pen name, has just released her first two books in 2023, I'll Always Love You, and Back to You, in Sunset Beach stories. She is planning this to become a multiple-book series.

A lifelong organic vegetable and flower gardener, Sharon and her husband lived for fifty years in the Wine Country of Northern California, where many of her stories take place. Recently, they have moved to the beautiful Gulf Coast of Florida, with stories of shipwrecks, the white sugar-sand beaches of Sunset, Treasure Island and Indian Rocks Beaches.

She loves hearing from fans through her website: authorsharonhamilton.com

Find out more about Sharon, her upcoming releases, appearances and news when you sign up for Sharon's newsletter.

Facebook:
facebook.com/SharonHamiltonAuthor

Twitter:
twitter.com/sharonlhamilton

Pinterest:

pinterest.com/AuthorSharonH

Amazon:
amazon.com/Sharon-Hamilton/e/B004FQQMAC

BookBub:
bookbub.com/authors/sharon-hamilton

Youtube:
youtube.com/channel/UCDInkxXFpXp_4Vnq08ZxM
BQ

Soundcloud:
soundcloud.com/sharon-hamilton-1

Sharon Hamilton's Rockin' Romance Readers:
facebook.com/groups/sealteamromance

Sharon Hamilton's Goodreads Group:
goodreads.com/group/show/199125-sharon-hamilton-
readers-group

Visit Sharon's Online Store:
sharon-hamilton-author.myshopify.com

Life is one fool thing after another.
Love is two fool things after each other.

REVIEWS

PRAISE FOR THE
SEAL BROTHERHOOD SERIES

"Fans of Navy SEAL romance, I found a new author to feed your addiction. Finely written and loaded delicious with moments, Sharon Hamilton's storytelling satisfies like a thick bar of chocolate." —Marliss Melton, bestselling author of the *Team Twelve* Navy SEALs series

"Sharon Hamilton does an EXCELLENT job of fitting all the characters into a brotherhood of SEALS that may not be real but sure makes you feel that you have entered the circle and security of their world. The stories intertwine with each book before...and each book after and THAT is what makes Sharon Hamilton's SEAL Brotherhood Series so very interesting. You won't want to put down ANY of her books and they will keep you reading into the night when you should be sleeping. Start with this book...and you will not want to stop until you've read the whole series and then...you will be waiting for Sharon to write the next one." (5 Star Review)

"Kyle and Christy explode all over the pages in this first book, *[Accidental SEAL]*, in a whole new series of SEALs. If the twist and turns don't get your heart jumping, then maybe the suspense will. This is a must read for those that are looking for love and adventure with a little sloppy love thrown in for good measure." (5 Star Review)

PRAISE FOR THE
BAD BOYS OF SEAL TEAM 3 SERIES

"I love reading this series! Once you start these books, you can hardly put them down. The mix of romance and suspense keeps you turning the pages one right after another! Can't wait until the next book!" (5 Star Review)

"I love all of Sharon's Seal books, but *[SEAL's Code]* may just be her best to date. Danny and Luci's journey is filled with a wonderful insight into the Native American life. It is a love story that will fill you with warmth and contentment. You will enjoy Danny's journey to become a SEAL and his reasons for it. Good job Sharon!" (5 Star Review)

PRAISE FOR THE
BAND OF BACHELORS SERIES

"*[Lucas]* was the first book in the Band of Bachelors series and it was a phenomenal start. I loved how we got to see the other SEALs we all love and we got a look at Lucas and Marcy. They had an instant attraction, and their love was very intense. This book had it all, suspense, steamy romance, humor, everything you want in a riveting, outstanding read. I can't wait to read the next book in this series." (5 Star Review)

PRAISE FOR THE
TRUE BLUE SEALS SERIES

"Keep the tissues box nearby as you read *True Blue SEALs: Zak* by Sharon Hamilton. I imagine more than I wish to that the circumstances surrounding Zak and Amy are all too real for returning military personnel and their families. Ms. Hamilton has put us right in the middle of struggles and successes that these two high school sweethearts endure. I have read several of Sharon Hamilton's military romances but will say this is the most emotionally intense of the ones that I have read. This is a well-written, realistic story with authentic characters that will have you rooting for them and proud of those who serve to keep us safe. This is an author who writes amazing stories that you love and cry with the characters. Fans of Jessica Scott and Marliss Melton will want to add Sharon Hamilton to their list of realistic military romance writers." (5 Star Review)

PRAISE FOR THE
GOLDEN VAMPIRES OF TUSCANY SERIES

"Well to say the least I was thoroughly surprised. I have read many Vampire books, from Ann Rice to Kym Grosso and a few other Authors, so yes I do like Vampires, not the super scary ones from the old days, but the new ones are far more interesting, far more human than one can remember. I found Honeymoon Bite a totally engrossing book, I was not able to put it down, page after page I found delight, love, understanding, well that is until the bad bad Vamp started being really bad. But seeing someone love another person so much that they would do anything to protect them, well that had me going, then well there was more and for a while I thought it was the end of a beautiful love story that spanned not only time but, spanned Italy and California. Won't divulge how it ended, but I did shed a few tears after screaming but Sharon Hamilton did not let me down, she took me on amazing trip that I loved, look forward to reading another Vampire book of hers."

"An excellent paranormal romance that was exciting, romantic, entertaining and very satisfying to read. It had me anticipating what would happen next many times over, so much so I could not put it down and even finished it up in a day. The vampires in this book were different from your average vampire, but I enjoy different variations and changes to the same old stuff. It made for a more unpredictable read and more adventurous to explore! Vampire lovers, any paranormal readers and even those who love the romance genre will enjoy Honeymoon Bite."

"This is the first non-Seal book of this author's I have read and I loved it. There is a cast-like hierarchy in this vampire community with humans at the very bottom and Golden vampires at the top. Lionel is a dark vampire who are servants of the Goldens. Phoebe is a Golden who has not decided if she will remain human or accept the turning to become a vampire. Either way she and Lionel can never be together since it is forbidden.

I enjoyed this story and I am looking forward to the next installment."

"A hauntingly romantic read. Old love lost and new love found. Family, heart, intrigue and vampires. Grabbed my attention and couldn't put down. Would definitely recommend."

"Dear FATHER IN HEAVEN,

If I may respectfully say so sometimes you are a strange God. Though you love all mankind,

It seems you have special predilections too.

You seem to love those men who can stand up alone who face impossible odds, who challenge every bully and every tyrant ~

Those men who know the heat and loneliness of Calvary. Possibly you cherish men of this stamp because you recognize the mark of your only son in them.

Since this unique group of men known as the SEALs know Calvary and suffering, teach them now the mystery of the resurrection ~ that they are indestructible, that they will live forever because of their deep faith in you.

And when they do come to heaven, may I respectfully warn you, Dear Father, they also know how to celebrate. So please be ready for them when they insert under your pearly gates.

Bless them, their devoted Families and their Country on this glorious occasion.

We ask this through the merits of your Son, Christ Jesus the Lord, Amen."

By Reverend E.J. McMalhon S.J. LCDR, CHC, USN
Awards Ceremony SEAL Team One
1975 At NAB, Coronado